Deadbeat

Charles Ray

North Potomac, MD

This book is a work of fiction. Names, descriptions, places, and incidents are products of the author's imagination, or are used fictionally. Any resemblance to actual events or persons, living or dead, is purely coincidental.

For information about this and other works of this author, contact the author at charlesray.author@yahoo.com.

Printed in the United States of America.

ISBN: 0692247866
ISBN-13: 978-0692247860

What readers have to say about Al Pennyback mysteries

Death From Unnatural Causes
"The flow of the plot was everything a mystery should be." – Joseph L. Chastain

Death in White Satin
" . . .it becomes a page turner to find out what happens next." – FiretalkerPR

Death and Taxis
"This was a nice easy read with brilliantly fleshed out characters." – Joe Warshowsky

Deadly Paradise
" . . .a light and easy summertime read." – Sherry Fundin

If I Should Die Before I Wake
"I would never have guessed the ending." – Drea Buczeskie

Dead Men Don't Answer
"Never a dull moment . ." – Sandra Emery

Till Death Do Us Part
" . . .believable. It kept my attention. . ." – Michael McMullen

1.

A man always takes full responsibility for his actions. That's what Uncle Buddy used to say to us boys who followed him around all the time, hanging on his every word. Uncle Buddy was something of an enigma. I don't remember when he came to town, he just showed up one day. He never told us where he came from, but from the way he talked we knew he wasn't from East Texas. He didn't have that slow, sugary drawl that everyone else had, and he spoke at a faster clip. But, he knew how to bait a hook, could shoot hickory nuts out of a tree from fifty yards, and knew more stories than a bunch of adolescent boys from a small farm town ever knew existed. My buddies and I hung around him, and our parents didn't mind, because they knew he always taught us to be responsible, never cursed in our presence, and would conk or thump our noggins with his calloused index finger whenever he caught us misbehaving. This was in the 1950s before corporal punishment became taboo, and when any adult was considered responsible for any child within his or her reach.

Uncle Buddy wasn't really my uncle, and his name wasn't Buddy. I didn't know that, of course, until just before I graduated from high school. He died that year. Just went to bed in the little two room shack that he'd built himself, and never woke up. One of his neighbors found the body when the place started to stink.

They had a big funeral for him. Every black person in town came, and even a few of the white farmers for whom he occasionally did odd jobs came and sat in the back of the little white frame church that was filled to capacity.

I remember it vividly because it was in early April, and it had already started to get hot – not hot like it gets in the summer, but hot enough that sitting in a packed building with nothing but little paper fans flapping ineffectually and moving the warm around that you're soaking wet pretty quick. I also remember it because that was the day I discovered who Uncle Buddy really was.

His real name was Oscar Perlmutter. They had it printed in real fancy letters on the mimeographed program that was handed out to everyone as they entered the church. That day, sitting in a middle pew in that hot church, I finally learned his name. The program also had a blurry picture of him as a much younger man wearing a military uniform. Back home after the service, when I asked my dad about it, he told me what he knew. Oscar had originally come from St. Louis, Missouri, where he'd lived since coming home from World War II. He'd originally come from a little town in Oregon, but while in a military hospital recovering from wounds he'd sustained driving supplies across Germany for Patton's Third Army, he'd met a black nurse, one of the few in England at the time, and when he was demobilized, he followed her to St. Louis. My dad didn't know her name. He said Oscar would never speak it, and looked pained whenever he talked about her, which was seldom. I know he never told us kids her name – or anything else about his past.

He'd planned to marry her, though. That much he did tell my dad. He also told him why they never wed. A week before the wedding, his fiancée was coming home from the local black=owned hospital where she worked as a nurse supervisor. She'd had the night shift in the ER. As she was crossing the street a block from the apartment they shared, a driver came careening around the corner in a pickup truck. She was knocked twenty feet to land a in a crumpled and bleeding heap on the sidewalk. The paramedics pronounced her dead at the scene. The pickup driver drove away, but not before Oscar, who had been attracted by the sound of screaming - the other pedestrians who had witnessed the accident – came out of the apartment just as the truck was speeding away. He got a good look at the driver, a middle aged white man in a plaid shirt and overalls, with a frightened look on his sunburned face. He also got a good look at the vehicle's plate number.

It took him a week, but he eventually found a janitor who worked nights in the Department of Motor Vehicles. The man let him in one night, and he broke into the records section and spent half the night going through filing cabinets until he found the man's name and address. The next night he paid the man a visit. He was a farmer who lived alone on a small farm just outside the city, so it was an easy matter for Oscar to break a window in the kitchen of the run down frame house, enter and catch the man unawares in his bed. At first, he tried to put up a fight, but Oscar had thirty pounds and a lot of anger on him. He beat the man until he wasn't moving, and left him lying still and bleeding on his bedroom floor.

Knowing it would just be a matter of time until the police identified him, and thinking he'd killed the man, Oscar went back to his apartment, packed what he could carry in his old army duffel bag, and hit the road. He hitchhiked and walked until he crossed the Red River and entered the back country of East Texas, an area of small towns, farms and oil derricks, crisscrossed by two lane blacktop roads and red clay dirt roads, with more dogs and wildlife than people, where people would nod and say hello, but wouldn't engage a stranger in conversation if he didn't want to talk.

That was all I knew about Uncle Buddy aka Oscar Perlmutter. But, for reasons I could never explain, in April sometimes memories of him would pop into my mind. Maybe it was the heat reminding me of East Texas. Warm weather had come early to Washington, DC, and the air conditioner in my office was straining to cool the lukewarm air. My shirt had dark half-moon stains at the armpits from sweat. It wasn't exactly uncomfortable to me – I'd suffered much hotter Aprils as a kid growing up - but I knew that Heather Bunche, my assistant and partner, was sitting at her desk flapping a paper fan for all it was worth. The woman hates to sweat.

I suppose you're wondering who the heck I am, right? My name is Al Pennyback – actually Alfred Einstein Pennyback, thanks to a mother who was a great fan of the German scientist, and who lived in a culture where giving your kids wacky names was all too common, and where everyone was usually called by their first and middle names. By the time I was in junior high, though, no one called me Alfred Einstein. I'd become pretty good with my fists, and was big for my age, so from eighth grade, I was just Al. Now and then I'd run into some idiot who'd insist on calling me Albert, but a glare from my dark brown eyes was usually enough to set them straight. If that didn't work, I'd ball up my fists, their knuckles swollen from years of studying and practicing karate and taekwondo, and flex my chest muscles, and they'd get the hint. Actually, I prefer strangers just calling me Mr. Pennyback. I've never been all that comfortable jumping into using first names too early after meeting someone.

I'm a private investigator. Have been for more than a decade, ever since I retired from the army after my wife, Sarah, and my son, Ethan, were killed, along with the members of Ethan's elementary school soccer team, by a truck driver who ran a stop sign and T-boned the van Sarah was driving, bringing them back from an evening soccer match in Arlington.

That put me in a funk for a while, but my friend Quincy Chang, a former army JAG lawyer, now a partner in a DC law firm, talked me into getting my PI license and set me up with a ten thousand buck a month retainer from his firm. The work for the firm is easy – chasing clients who fail to pay their fees, or locating lost heirs to obscure fortunes – leaving me time to take the occasional over the transom case.

Many of these cases are brought in by Heather. She collects people with problems the way a black dress collects lint. We charge a variable rate depending on the client's ability to pay – and from time to time even take a case pro bono. The main criteria for me to accept the case, besides the person really needing help, is that it has to involve a puzzle. The harder the puzzle the better I like it. I can never resist a puzzle. Like some people who can't ignore a ringing phone, I can't ignore an unsolved puzzle. These cases didn't bring in much money, usually just enough to cover the office's utilities, but with the retainer and my army retirement pay, we get by.

My mind was moving on from Uncle Buddy to my plans for the weekend when Heather walked into my office.

"Hey, honey bunch," I said, using the pet name she wouldn't let anyone else but me use. "What's up? Tired of sweating out there, and want to join me in here where it's cooler?"

That was meant to be a joke. My office is on the west side of the building, and it was three in the afternoon, so even with the blinds almost closed, it resembled a sauna or a steam bath – I could never decide which. She didn't laugh. She hardly ever laughs at my jokes.

"There's someone here who needs to talk to you," she said. "She wants to hire you."

I gave her one of my 'right eyebrow' lifted looks – the one meant to convey skepticism. She ignored that just like she ignores my jokes.

She was being unreadable, which led me to think I wouldn't be happy about the case.

"Heather, you know we don't do divorce cases."

"Did I say it was a divorce case?" Now, her eyebrows were arched upward. "No one said anything about a divorce case."

Methinks she did protest too much. There had to be something fishy about it. I have a sense about such things. On the other hand, I had made an assumption and jumped to a conclusion with no evidence to support it, something I'd often told Heather a good investigator never does, so she'd been right to be upset.

"Okay, I stand chastised," I said. "Who is she, and what does she want to hire me for?"

"I think I should let her tell you that," Heather said. She stepped aside, pushing the door open wider.

A woman who was almost my six-one in height, with close-cropped, jet black hair framing a cocoa-colored oval face which was dominated by a pair of the largest, darkest, and most soulful eyes I'd ever seen glided in. She was wearing a shimmery blue blouse that clung to a pair of perfect breasts that from the sway weren't encumbered by a bra, and a matching blue skirt that stopped midway down a pair of smooth brown thighs that would cause the temperature in a meat locker to rise. I'm a one-woman man, and at the moment Sandra Winter, a teacher at Carter High School, one of DC's inner city schools, is that woman, but I'm neither blind nor dead. I can still appreciate beauty, and this woman was a beauty.

I stood and moved to the side of my desk, extending my hand. She grasped it with a grip that was smooth, dry, warm, and firm. Her eyes locked with mine. She seemed to be peering into my soul. *"I'll have to watch myself with this one,"* I thought. I'd let myself slip once, with a beautiful singer who I was acting as a bodyguard for, and had made a promise to myself that I'd never do that again.

"Mr. Pennyback, I have a problem, and Heather says you're the man to help me solve it," she said in a voice that was smoky and husky like an aged scotch whiskey.

"I have been known to solve problems," I said. "Why don't you have a seat and tell me what yours is."

I motioned for Heather to leave. Not that I needed – or wanted – to be alone with such a beautiful woman. I have all the woman I need in Sandra Winter, who has been living with me for a few years now. But, three people in my tiny office would raise the temperature to an uncomfortable level until the building air conditioning system resumed working. Besides, I only have two chairs – a scuffed leather executive chair I got at a military surplus auction that I sit in, and a wooden chair that I keep beside the desk, which I mostly use to keep files off the desk itself. It was empty. We hadn't had much to work on for a while.

Heather gave me a smirk and withdrew to the outer office, closing the door as she left.

"I suppose I should start by telling you my name," she said. "Candace, Candace Kaine. I work as a sales clerk at Marshalls, downtown in the National Press Building."

"A pleasure meeting you, uh, Ms. Kaine. Now, tell me your problem."

"Call me Candy," she said.

I held back a laugh. Candy Kaine! It was a name tailor-made for plays on words She did look sweet, though. "Okay, Candy," I said. "How can I help you?"

"I want you to find someone for me."

A missing person. That was what I did for Holcombe, Stein and Chang. Unless the person had left the country, it didn't sound too complicated.

"Who is this missing person, and how long has he . . . or she . . . been missing?"

"*He* has been gone for three weeks now," she said. "His name is Christopher Cross, and he's my baby's father."

2.

A part of my mind was processing her name and the missing dude's name, and trying to keep me from making some smart ass remark, while the rest was taking in the story she told me.

You have to give me a break here. You must admit that Candy Kaine and Chris Cross aren't exactly your garden variety names – at least, in all the years I'd been a gumshoe, it was a first for me. It made my moniker seem lame – I wondered if their respective parents were as aware of what they were doing to them as my mother had been when she named me.

I took a steno pad from my desk drawer and made notes as she talked. I figured if my hands were busy, they might keep my brain from allowing my mouth to do something dumb or even hurtful.

"Chris and I started going out together when

we were in high school," she said. "He quit in eleventh grade, and we broke it off for a couple of years, but then shortly after I graduated, he showed up at my apartment one night, and we've been living together ever since – that's like a bit over six years now. We got a kid, a boy named Calvin, and he looks just like his daddy."

"You two have a problem – an argument, or something?" I asked.

"No, we were getting along just fine. 'Bout a month ago, though, Chris started acting kind of funny, and then three weeks ago, he said he was going out to get cigarettes, and that's the last time I saw him."

Sounded to me like a guy who'd gotten all he wanted from her and decided to go graze in another pasture. Unfortunately, such behavior is all too common – a woman lets a man live with her without benefit of a marriage license, and one day he decides to relocate, leaving her holding the bag . . . and the baby or babies.

"If I'm going to find him, I'll need to know as much as possible about him," I said. "Like, where he worked, his favorite hangouts . . . oh, and I'll need a recent photo of him."

She reached into the little pearl-studded bag she carried and took out a strip of those photos you can get done at the booths at carnivals. There were three photos, two of a smarmily handsome light brown skinned man with her, and one of him with a little boy who looked like a younger clone. I took the photos and put them on my desk.

"Those were taken last year. We spent the weekend at Ocean City for Calvin's fifth birthday."

"Your son is a handsome boy," I said. "Now, where does Chris work?"

She blinked. And then she looked at me kind of wide-eyed and innocent.

"Well . . . I'm . . . not . . . really . . . sure."

Now it was my turn to look wide-eyed, but my gaze was far from innocent.

"You mean he lived off you all that time?" I couldn't keep the shock from my voice.

Her wide eyes narrowed to little slits, and her luscious lips curved downward.

"No, he did not," she said. "Chris paid half the rent, bought the food, presents for Calvin, and he paid for our little trips, like the one to Ocean City."

"But, you don't know where his money came from?"

"Uh, he did odd jobs, you know. He was smart, but because he didn't have his high school diploma it was hard for him to get signed on for a regular job."

This was beginning not to sound good. A high school dropout with no steady job, but with plenty of walking around money had the smell of illegal activity to it. A little voice in the recesses of my brain was telling me to walk away from this one, but those soulful dark eyes of hers, with the unshed tears lingering in the corners threatening to spill down those smooth cheeks was asking for my help. I figured it wouldn't hurt to look for the guy. But, I needed more information on the needle before jumping into the haystack.

"Does he have a passport?" I asked.

"I don't know," she answered.

"What about his favorite hangouts?"

She shrugged. "He liked a beer now and then, but I don't drink, so I never went with him to wherever it is he went to drink."

"Did he have any particular friends he hung out with?"

"I told you, I never went with him when he went out to drink. I never heard him talk about anyone in particular, though."

She didn't seem to know much about the man – except that she loved him. That much I saw in her eyes when she spoke his name. The body language in the photos told me that he loved her and the kid too. What it didn't tell me was why he'd up and disappear. That was a puzzle, and I'm a sucker for a puzzle.

"Okay," I said. "You haven't given me much to go on, but I could give it a shot. No guarantees, mind you. Now, our usual fee is five hundred a day plus expenses." She gasped. "But, I'm sure Heather has told you that we can make special arrangements for some clients."

"I . . . I'm willing to pay, but I can't afford that much."

Even though she was a sales clerk in a big fancy store, her salary and commissions probably didn't come to all that much. And now, of course, with half the income gone, she had to pick up all the expenses.

"How about fifty bucks a day and expenses," I said. "And, you can pay on installment."

She smiled at me. It was a smile that could melt the polar ice cap. I don't know what she saw in Chris Cross, but I could certainly see what he saw in her.

"That sounds fine," she said. "Oh, just one more thing – Calvin's birthday is May 10, and when I asked him what gift he wanted, he said all he wants is his daddy back. I hope you can find Chris before May 10. It would mean so much to a little boy."

That's what I like on a case – no pressure.

After puzzles, the next thing I'm a sucker for is kids, and when the two come together like this, it makes it interesting.

"Great. You go on out, and Sandra will prepare a contract for you to sign."

"You'll start on the case right away?" There was surprise in her voice.

I showed her my notebook. She probably couldn't read my crabby writing, but I had been taking notes the whole time we were talking.

"I've already started," I said.

3.

Candy Kaine left my office at a quarter past eleven. As soon as she'd gone I called Buster Mayweather, one of my best friends, and a detective with the Washington Metropolitan Police Department, and asked him to meet me at Mom's, our favorite hangout, for lunch.

While I normally drive to Mom's, which is on Sixteenth Street near U, Kaine and Cross's apartment was on Fourteenth Street just north of T, so I thought I'd get to know the neighborhood and get some exercise in the bargain by taking the Green Line Metro from Waterfront to U Street Cardoza and walking to Mom's. It was a three block trek from the Metro station to Mom's, and the combination of mid-day heat and humidity had me sweating by the time I got there.

Mom's is something of an institution in the area. A soul food restaurant, it had been at the same location with several name changes for more than forty years. Word was it had been one of the few buildings to survive the riots that broke out after the announcement of Dr. Martin Luther King, Jr's assassination. The rioters allegedly stopped their burning and looting at noon and dropped into Mom's for a lunch of fried chicken, biscuits and gravy. While the stories might be fables, Mom's appearance made me believe it.

Just over five-six, Mom must weigh three hundred pounds. And, it's evenly distributed. She has broad shoulders, humongous breasts, hips a yard wide, and legs like carved mahogany columns. She's given to wearing one-piece flowery dresses that look like they're about to burst at the seams, over which she wears an apron big enough to serve as a two-man tent. She smiles a lot, but there's a no-bullshit tone in her voice and a glint in her eye that leaves you in no doubt that this is a woman you don't mess with. Mom's is run like boot camp, and she's meaner than any drill sergeant I've ever known. But, the food is great.

She was sitting at her usual place on a stool near the cash register at the end of the counter when I walked in. When she saw me she smiled, but her smile quickly turned into a look of concern.

"Lordy mercy, child," she said. "You look like you done been rode hard and put up wet. You been walkin' out there in that heat?"

"Yeah, Mom. I walked from the U Street-Cardoza station."

"Boy, are you crazy? You gone git yourself heat stroke. Your car broke down?"

"No," I said. "I just felt like walking."

I'd walked through worse. Heck, as a kid growing up in East Texas, I'd walked to school when the temperature was in triple digits, and our school at the time didn't have air conditioning. At least Mom's was comfortably cool. I could feel that sweat evaporating. Along with the woody smells of some kind of meat being fried, and the yeasty smell of biscuits, it was comforting.

"Well, that no good Buster already here." She pointed to Buster, who was sitting at our usual table in the corner near the big plate glass window hunched over a plate of chicken, mashed potatoes and biscuits. "You gone and set down and I'll bring you a big glass of ice tea just the way you like it."

"Thanks, Mom. I'll take the tea with lunch. First, though, bring me a big mug of hot, black coffee."

"Why you want to drink hot coffee, sweating like that? You oughta drink something cold to cool off."

"Trust me, hot coffee will help me cool off."

Most people mistakenly think that drinking cold liquids when you're hot is how to cool down. It's just the opposite. The hot liquid in your gut causes your body to try and lower its temperature, while cold drinks do just the opposite. Mom looked skeptical, but, like Buster, she'd become accustomed to the fact that I knew a lot of really strange things.

"Okay, if you say so. Now, gone and sit down."

I walked over and took my usual chair with my back against the wall and a view of the front door and the sidewalk outside. Buster looked up at me with his mouth full of food and grunted something.

Mom brought me a large white mug full of hot black coffee flavored with chicory. I took a big swallow. It burned my mouth a little, but as it went down I could feel my body temperature dropping.

Buster swallowed, and wiped his mouth daintily with a napkin. I laughed. It looked so funny – a big, bald, black man with a Fu Manchu mustache and the shoulder and chest muscles of a football linebacker, which is what he would have been if he hadn't blown his knee out in college, daintily wiping his lips. He frowned at me.

"What's so funny?" he asked.

I didn't think he'd get it, so I just shook my head.

"I was just thinking about my latest case," I said. I told him about it, especially the names, Chris Cross and Candy Kaine.

He saw the humor, and joined me in the laughter. "So," he said. "You gone find a dude named Chris Cross for a babe named Candy Kaine? Bro, you've had some weird cases, but this one's a pip."

"Tell me about it. I'm gonna need your help on this one, Buster."

"You payin' for lunch?"

"Sure, lunch is on me," I said.

"In that case, just tell me what you need," he said.

Charles Ray

4.

After Buster and I finished our fried chicken lunch and wiped the grease from our faces, he went back to his precinct and I walked over to Fourteenth Street.

I'd cooled off while I was in Mom's, but the mercury had gone up, so by the time I got to Candace Kaine's neighborhood I could feel the sweat dripping from my armpits, and my shirt was sticking to my body. It reminded me of the weather in East Texas, minus the mosquitos and other bugs that dive bomb you every few seconds, sucking your blood and leaving large red welts on any exposed skin.

The building that she lived in was actually closer to Thirteenth Street than fourteenth, a stretch of T Street where two to four story brick townhouses, some converted into apartment buildings with four to six units, lined both sides. All of the buildings were jammed together, wall to wall, with postage stamp squares of scraggly grass in front, and a slightly larger walled-in space in back where garbage cans were kept. The building was gray brick, or had been. Years of pollution had turned the gray bricks a sooty color that wasn't quite black, but almost.

I passed a beefy guy dressed in worker's coveralls, who ignored me and checked his watch. Across the street another guy in similar coveralls stood near the bus stop, also checking his watch. Both were young, looking to be in their late twenties. Their dark scowling faces didn't exactly invite conversation. It didn't matter to me, because they weren't what I was looking for. Just ahead, though, I did see what I was looking for. I wanted someone who paid attention to what was going on in the area – someone with nowhere to go and little to do besides sit and watch. It might be considered stereotyping, but that meant an older person, preferably someone who was retired with nothing but time on his or her hands.

An elderly man, his dark brown skin furrowed and cracked, sat on the stoop of the building next to Kaine's. He leaned back against the red brick, his head moving slowly from side to side as he watched the traffic zip past. His watery brown eyes didn't exactly lock on me, but I could tell that he was watching me as I approached. I stopped near him, my shadow covering his bent frame.

He squinted up at me. His look was neither friendly nor unfriendly. "You lookin' for somebody?" he asked.

"Yes," I said. I showed him my PI ID. "I'm trying to locate Christopher Cross. I understand he lives here."

"Not here – next door. Why you lookin' for him? He do somethin' wrong?"

If you want to know what's going on in a neighborhood, find a retired person, usually a man, and ask. The key is to keep from letting yourself get snookered into a situation where you're telling more about yourself than you're learning. These old guys have nothing but time on their hands, and they get bored. You don't want to piss them off, though, so you have to figure a way to make it look like you're telling them things, but you're actually interrogating them.

"We private eyes have to be discrete, you know," I said. "Client confidentiality and all, you understand." I leaned forward as I spoke, keeping my voice low. His head bobbed up and down.

"That boy in some kinda trouble?"

"Has he been in trouble before?"

"Naw, but I figure it's just a matter of time," he said. "He pretty tight 'bout what he do, but I know he up to something no good."

31

"Really? I hadn't heard that he was doing anything illegal."

"Now, fella, I didn't say nothin' 'bout illegal – I said I think he up to no good."

"What's the difference?" I asked. I gave him my best innocent look.

"You ain't from 'round here," he said. "Else you'd know what I mean. I don't mean he dealin' drugs or nothin' like that. But, I think he be runnin' 'round and gettin' money from folk under false pretense, know what I mean."

His idea of the line between behavior that was illegal, and behavior that was just 'no good' was different than mine.

"You saying he runs scams on people?"

"That's a harsh way to put it," he said. "But the boy always got money in his pocket, and he ain't got no job that anybody can see. If he ain't runnin' hos or sellin' crack, how else he gone get his hands on money?"

"Has he ever been in trouble with the police?"

"I don't think so," he said.

"Then, you don't really *know* that he's in any kind of trouble."

"Naw, I don't *know* it, but I got a feelin' 'bout it, and I ain't usually wrong."

"I'm just trying to understand," I said. "If I'm gonna find him, I need to know as much as possible. Tell me, what causes you to have the feeling he might be in trouble?"

"Well, I ain't seen him around for a while, and that strange, 'cause he always take that little boy of his to the park down the street in the afternoons. He do love that boy, I tell you. He ain't like some of the other deadbeats what screw the girls 'round here, and after they drop the brats, hit the road. The other thing is, you the second to come asking where he is, and the other men what asked looked like trouble."

Charles Ray

5.

The old man couldn't tell me much more than the two men who'd been in the neighborhood the day before weren't cops or private detectives, and they looked tough and mean. My curiosity was aroused. I wasn't the only one looking for Chris Cross. I wondered why.

I walked the block to the U Street-Cardoza Metro station. The Yellow Line train was first in the station, which meant a change of trains at L'Enfant Plaza to the Green Line, but the next Green Line Train wasn't for fifteen minutes. I got on the train, which was nearly empty. That would change, I knew, in an hour when the rush of people leaving their downtown jobs to their homes in suburbia or the outer rim city neighborhoods began.

At L'Enfant Plaza, I got off and stood back from the edge of the platform to wait for the next Green Line train, wondering why I didn't just do that at U Street. The other side of the platform, passengers heading north toward Prince Georges County, Maryland, had about fifteen people, with a few more coming down the escalator. My side had me and two guys who looked like workers. They were farther down the platform, their heads together in conversation. I didn't pay them any attention. That's the metro protocol. People think New York City is the most impersonal city in the U.S., but they've never been to DC. It might be a southern city geographically, but people here inhabit their own little personal bubbles, admitting entry only to those they know – except for the grifters looking for handouts.

The red lights at the platform edge started blinking, signaling that the train was approaching. I'd picked a good spot. When the train slid to a stop, I was just to the side of the doors to an empty car. When the doors whispered open I entered and took one of the inward facing seats – one of the few that didn't have crumpled newspapers or food wrappers on it, and settled back for the short ride to Waterfront.

"Green Line train to Branch Avenue," the scratchy voice announced. "Next stop,

Waterfront-SEU. Thank you for riding Metro."

When the train came out of the tunnel and came to a jerky stop, a woman's voice announced that the doors were opening, and people on the platform should allow passengers to depart the train before trying to board. There weren't more than ten people on the platform, all in a cluster at the door I was exiting. I politely pushed past a fat woman who had ignored the announcement and was trying to get her bulk through the door before I could get out, getting a scowl for my effort.

"When entering, please move to the center of the car," the disembodied voice said.

I made my way to the escalator. As I stepped on it, one of the beefy workers walked past me and moved to the right, resting his buttocks against the rubber railing. The other guy got on and stopped a few steps behind me.

The escalator made screeching sounds as it bore us upward to the parking lot of the shopping center in which the metro entrance was located.

I was lost in thought, lulled by the swaying of the escalator's slow upward journey. As it reached the top, and I stepped off, I noticed that the worker ahead of me had stopped a few feet away and turned in my direction, his right hand in the pocket of his coveralls. He had a leering smile on his dark face. I then felt a pressure in the small of my back.

"Don't turn around," a rough voice said behind me. "Just walk slowly forward and follow my friend."

The pressure in my back was unmistakable – the business end of some kind of small pistol. The guy in front turned and walked to his left toward the corner of the drugstore that formed the right side of an open square. He then turned left along the cracked sidewalk, and left again toward the rear of the building. I kept my hands loosely at my side and followed him into the weed-strewn vacant lot at the rear of the building.

The guy behind me grabbed my shoulder and shoved me against the rough brick wall. He had a Saturday night special in his hand, which he pointed at my face. His friend took one from his pocket, holding it loosely at his side.

"If you guys are planning to rob me," I said. "You're in for a disappointment. I've only got twenty bucks in my wallet."

They laughed – harsh and guttural. I didn't like the sound of that.

"We don't want your fuckin' money, dude," the guy with the gun in my face said. "We want to know what you doin' lookin' for that little turd Chris Cross."

That triggered an image in my brain. I'd

been so focused on the case, I'd been inattentive. This guy was the beefy goon at the bus stop, and his friend was the one I'd passed near Kaine's building. I'd been concentrating so on my conversation with the old man I hadn't noticed them. One of them had probably overheard it, and they'd followed me all the way from Cardoza.

"You mind telling me why you're concerned about it?" I asked. "I'm a private investigator, and what I do is between me and my client."

"Oh yeah – who your client?" the other guy asked.

"That, I'm afraid, is also privileged information."

They looked at each other, confusion on their faces. The one nearest me lifted his pistol, resting the barrel on the end of my nose and pulling the hammer back.

"Well now, friend," he said. "Maybe we just gone beat the privilege out of you. How you like that?"

"I wouldn't like that at all," I said. I moved my head to the side, and whipped my left hand up jamming my thumb into the space between the hammer and firing plate. I twisted sharply, ripping the pistol from his hand.

Before he could react with more than an angry and surprised snarl, I punched the bridge of his nose with my right hand, and spinning, I swung my right foot up into his friend's crotch. He made a mewing sound, grabbed at his crouch and dropped to the ground, curing up into a fetal position. I turned back to the first man who was holding both hands over his bleeding nose, his eyes crossed trying to see the damage my fist had done. I punched him in the sternum, and when he dropped his hands to grab at his chest, I popped him on the point of the chin, snapping his head back and sending him toppling like a felled tree.

I retrieved the two pistols and emptied them. Walking over to a nearby trash can, I dropped pistols and bullets in, and walked off, never looking back.

When I returned to the shopping center parking lot, I pulled out my phone and dialed Buster. When he came on I told him what had happened, and gave him the address. Then I walked the three blocks to my office, whistling all the way.

6.

Buster called me about thirty minutes after I got back to the office.

"Hey, Al," he said. "The two guys were gone by the time the squad car got there, but the guns and ammo were in the trash can just like you said. We have the lab running the prints on 'em, so we ought to be able to ID these two stooges."

"When you pick 'em up," I said. "I'd be interested to know why they were so interested in Cross, or why they wanted to know why I was looking for him."

"Assuming you left 'em in any condition to talk," he said, laughing. "By the way, I got Christopher Cross's rap sheet. He's small time, but he's been busy."

"Funny, neither Kaine nor the old man in his neighborhood mentioned he had a

41

criminal record."

Buster laughed. "It's not exactly a *criminal* record, bro," he said. "Mostly a buncha reports on his behavior from just before and since he dropped out of school. He's been arrested a few times on misdemeanors, stuff like cheating old ladies out of their jewelry, but they always dropped the charges, so he's never really been convicted of anything."

"I thought juvie records were kept sealed."

"Yeah, technically they are, but I got a friend who works in juvenile court. He sent me the file on Cross on the QT, you know. And, I ran into an old buddy who works organized crime. Seems Cross's name came up in one of his investigations."

"Whoa, buddy," I said. "This guy jumped from petty misdemeanors to organized crime? How the hell did that happen?"

"He hasn't exactly become a made man or anything. But, he was reported to be involved somehow with Augie Manson, one of the up-and-comers in organized mob activity in the DC area. My friend didn't know how he was involved, but I thought you should know."

Cross was becoming more and more of an enigma. But, if he was tied up with the mob, I wasn't sure finding him was a good idea for Kaine or her son. I'd have to mull it over in my mind – and, dig up a few more facts – before approaching her with any such suggestion, though. If she still wanted me to find such a loser – well . . . the client is always right.

"Maybe I need to talk to this Manson character if I want to find Cross," I said.

"Hey, bro – I'm not sure that's such a bright idea. According to my friend, not much is known about Manson, but what is known ain't good. He's supposed to have a pretty short fuse, and he's got a lot of bad dudes workin' for him – dudes like the two you had the run-in with."

"I said maybe – I have a few other things to try before I take a step like that." Actually, I didn't have diddly squat, but Buster sounded serious. Maybe talking to a mobster wasn't my best idea. I'd keep my brain working until I came up with something else – maybe.

Buster breathed a sigh of relief that I could clearly hear over the phone. "Good," he said. "I'll keep seeing what I can dig up on this Cross dude."

Charles Ray

7.

Heather and I knocked off early, and I was at my home just off River Road in Montgomery County by 6:00. Sandra was already there. Her last class at Carter High School in the District had ended at 3:00, and for a change she had no after school activities to monitor.

It was Friday, and we'd planned to eat out. She'd showered, made up and dressed by the time I arrived, and was sitting on the sofa in the living room, looking like a picture from a fashion magazine – a bust hugging scooped neck pink blouse tucked into a purple skirt that stopped mid-thigh. She hopped up when I came in and rushed over to kiss me. As she did, she wrinkled her nose and made a face. I guess the layers of dried sweat got to her. I raised my right arm and sniffed. Okay, so there was a bit of a locker room smell, but I didn't think it was all that bad. What I thought, though, didn't matter. She stepped back and pointed toward the bathroom.

In the bathroom, I stripped down to the buff, dropping my clothes in the laundry hamper. I turned the shower on full, and turned the temperature up until it was as hot as I could stand. Like hot beverages, a hot shower also helps the body feel cooler. Counterintuitive, I know, but it works. I stood under the shower for a while, letting the hot water massage the tiredness from my muscles, and sluice off the grime and grit of the day. After soaping and scrubbing until my skin tingled, I had to admit, I felt – and smelt – better.

I toweled off and wrapped the damp towel around my waist while I brushed my teeth and shaved. My work in the bathroom completed, I went to the bedroom and dressed. I put on a light brown shirt and then pulled on a pair of brown khaki pants. Dark brown socks and brown loafers completed my ensemble. I didn't look like a male model, but at least I wouldn't look like some bum that Sandra had picked up on the street corner.

She whistled when I walked back into the living room, letting me know I'd chosen well.

"What does my lady fancy tonight – Korean, Chinese, or Thai?" I asked.

"You look so hot, I think Thai would be most appropriate," she said.

She had a wicked look in her bright blue eyes that said food wasn't the only hot thing she had in mind for the evening.

"Thai it is, babe."

There was a nice Thai place on Rockville Pike, not far from the White Flint Metro station in Rockville. We could get there without ever having to get on the I-495 Beltway, too, which was always a plus for me. The Beltway is rough during the day, but at night it's downright dangerous, with big semis hauling loads north and south, and motorists who overdrive their headlights or ability to respond. With that combination, accidents aren't a probability; they're a distinct possibility, and they tend to be deadly.

Rockville Pike at 7:45 in the evening – especially on Friday – is a crowded artery, but there are enough lights to keep speeds under Indy 500 rates. You only have to watch out for the idiots who change lanes at the last minute without signaling. We found a parking space in the lot adjacent to Thai Garden, not too far from the entrance.

Charles Ray

The place was dimly lit and crowded, but a beautiful woman, tall for a Thai, wearing a tight mid-thigh length skirt and strapless blouse, found us a table in the front corner. I convinced Sandra that wine wasn't appropriate with Thai food, so we ordered two bottles of *Singha* beer, which were brought right away. When it comes to Asian food Sandra always defers to me. She knows French and Mediterranean cuisine, but she's always nervous when it comes to Asian food. I ordered a plate of *som tam*, green mango salad, to start, *tom yang gung*, a shrimp soup with lemon grass and coconut milk, *larb moo*, minced pork with onions, dried pepper flakes, lime juice, and fish sauce, *pad krapao moo*, pork steamed with basil, *pad Thai*, fried noodles with prawns, and a large bowl of fragrant white rice.

Thai food doesn't take long to prepare, so we were only half done with our beer when it arrived. The aroma of lemon grass and coriander made my mouth water. The waitress serving us, a smaller but even prettier version of the one who'd seated us and taken our order, put a small wooden rack containing dried red pepper, sugar, salt, ground black pepper, fish sauce, and *prik kee new,* the little rat turd shaped Thai peppers, on the table. Sandra made a face when I took two of the peppers and put them on the side of my plate.

"You're not seriously considering eating those, are you?" she asked.

"Bet your bippy I am. I ate hotter peppers than these when I was a kid growing up in Texas. Besides, they add flavor."

She shook her head, causing her silky blonde hair to wave in front of her eyes. "I ate one once," she said. "It didn't add to the flavor – it burned so I couldn't taste the food."

I picked one of the little vegetables, whose name roughly translates in English to 'rat shit pepper', and popped it into my mouth. Sandra's had an incredulous look on her face as I began chewing. The pepper burned a little, but I put a spoonful of rice in and rolled it around in my mouth, which eased the burning.

"I used to do that when my detachment deployed to Thailand for exercises with the Thai army," I said. "The Thais got a real kick out of it. Besides, it's a good source of vitamin C."

She gave me that 'boys will be boys' look and began nibbling at the *som tam*. "I don't see why you need those peppers," she said after swallowing. "This salad is delicious, but it's pretty spicy all on its own."

A lot of Thai food is, but some people like the extra kick of the peppers. We made quick work of the salad, and started on the rest of the dishes, spooning a mound of white rice onto our plate, and then putting the other food around or on top of it – eating it with a fork and spoon in the Thai style.

We ate in silence for a while, washing the food down with beer. About halfway through the meal, I put my fork and spoon down and sat back.

"Sandra, babe," I said. "I have a question that I think only a woman can answer."

She looked mischievously at me over a spoonful of *larb moo*. "You want to know where babies *really* come from?"

"No, I think I solved that one. I have a question about relationships. Why would a reasonably intelligent, attractive woman chose to hook up with a loser?"

She put her spoon down and rested her chin on her steepled hands.

"That, my darling, is a good question," she said. "Believe it or not, that very question has been studied, but the conclusions are all over the place. Some researchers believe it's because some women are taught to believe that 'a good man is a good man' regardless of his educational or economic status. Then, of course, there are the women who will marry the first man who asks them for fear they'll never find another. That's sad, but probably not as sad as the women who feel that they must marry within their racial or ethnic group, regardless."

"Good grief. Women like that must end up having a pretty low opinion of themselves," I said.

"Many of them, unfortunately, start that way. They feel they're not worthy of getting man with their level of education or job, so they settle for whatever comes along."

I reached over and cupped her chin in my hand. "You wouldn't do anything like that, would you?"

"Hey, I settled for you, didn't I?

It took a few seconds for that to sink in. She saw understanding dawn in my eyes, and smiled broadly.

"Of course, I wouldn't, you ninny," she said.

"Don't do that, woman," I said. "You know how sensitive my ego is. Which reminds me, though, aren't there interpersonal problems in relationships between people with income or education gaps – especially, I would think, with men in a subordinate relationship."

"Yes, sometimes there's conflict. The

partner with less education or a lower paying job resents the other, and that leads to verbal or even physical abuse. You think that's the case with the woman who hired you?"

I wasn't sure what to think. Kaine's words and the pictures seemed to portray a close and loving relationship. I'd heard, though, that sometimes abused spouses and children cling closely to the abuser, seeking approval, or blaming themselves for the abuse. I didn't see any signs of physical abuse on her, but some chronic abusers are clever and do their dirty work on parts of the body not normally observed.

"I don't really know," I said. "She seems to love the guy, and from what I can gather so far, he's great with the kid. It's just that there's so much in this turkey's history – it makes me worry."

She took a sip of beer, and then daintily wiped her lips with the napkin, all the while her crystal blue eyes bored into me. I felt a tingling in my throat.

"Well, babe," she said. "Never underestimate the power of love. They say it can move mountains."

Maybe it can, but I wasn't sure it could bridge the gulf I was sensing between Kaine and Cross.

8.

Sandra's words were on my mind the next day as I sat behind my desk thinking about my next steps in the case.

I hadn't made any progress in finding Christopher Cross – I didn't even know where to start looking. People usually leave clues around all over the place, credit card receipts, sightings at stores or bars, something that gives you a starting point for tracking them down. Cross, though, had walked out of the Fourteenth Street building and seemingly disappeared – not even a puff of smoke.

I was staring at the photo of me with former-Chairman of the Joint Chiefs of Staff, General Colin Powell, taken during my assignment at the Pentagon, when Heather pushed the door open and poked her head in. She had a wide-eyed look of worry.

"Yeah, Heather, what's up?" I asked.

"Uh, boss, there's a guy here to see you."

"What does he want?"

"He won't say."

"Well then, tell him if he can't tell you what he wants, he can't see me."

She came fully into the office, followed by a man who looked as wide as he was tall. His dark blue suit looked like it would burst at the seams. He had skin that was a color that is hard to describe – part brown, part tan, part yellow – a square head with black hair that was heavily pomaded and brushed straight back from his high forehead in rippled waves, dark brown eyes that were set too close together in his large face, and fleshy lips that were formed into a pout or pucker.

"That, Mr. Pennyback, is not an option," he said in a gravelly voice.

I stood and moved around beside the desk, holding my clenched fists at my side.

"Who the hell are you," I asked. "And, by what right do you barge into my office like this?"

He laughed – a sound like pebbles in a tin

can. He was six inches shorter than me, but had me in girth, and up close, I could see that a lot of his bulk wasn't fat. He didn't look like he could move fast, but he did look like he could handle himself in a close quarters fight. He also had an overpowering smell of cheap cologne and pomade that caused my nose to itch.

"I am August Manson," he said. He stressed his name as if it should mean something to me. When I didn't react, he sighed. "I told your girl here that I had something important and confidential to discuss with you, but she ignored me."

"She's not my *girl*. Ms. Bunche is my partner," I said. "Anything you have to say to me you can say to her."

His cheeks darkened and puffed out. "Oh, I didn't know." He turned to Heather. "Such a sweet young thing is a . . . private detective. My, my, that is interesting. My apologies, young lady, I made a totally unwarranted assumption."

He took her hand in both his, and leaned forward as far as his girth would allow, kissing the back of her hand. Heather had a pained smile on her face until he released her hand.

"You're forgiven, Mr. Manson," she said.

"Please, my dear, call me Augie. All my friends call me Augie, and I do hope you and I can be friends."

She smiled shyly at him, but her eyes were on me, and they didn't have a happy look.

"Thank you," she said. "Will you talk to Mr. Manson, Al?"

"I suppose I might as well," I said.

"Well, you two will have to excuse me, I have work to do."

She backed out of the office, shooting me a querulous look as she left. I pointed at the chair beside my desk, hoping it wouldn't collapse under Manson's weight.

"Why don't you have a seat, and tell me what it is you want to talk about," I said.

He sat gingerly. The chair creaked, but held, and I breathed out slowly.

"Okay," he said. "Here's the deal. I understand you and I have something in common."

"Oh. I can't imagine what that would be."

"You're looking for Christopher Cross. I also would like to know Mr. Cross's whereabouts. I'm prepared to pay you for the information – if you've found him."

The image of two goons with guns came into my mind. I should have known they weren't after me on their own. So, Cross was involved with Manson. I hadn't held him in the highest esteem, but my opinion of him took a sharp dive with that realization.

"The problem with that is that I already have a client."

"By that I assume you're referring to the woman Cross was living with," he said. "I can assure you that I can pay you a lot more than she can."

"It's not a question of money."

"Oh, come on. It's always a question of money. I know Ms. Kaine is a fly chick, but she's just a department store clerk. I'm surprised she can even afford your fee. You tell me where Cross is when you find him, and I'll pay you ten thousand bucks."

For some, that much money would be a powerful motivation, but I was taught to keep my word, and I'd already signed an agreement with Candace Kaine.

"Sorry," I said. "No deal."

"Okay, twenty thousand."

Whatever his reason for wanting to find Cross, it was important. But, I wasn't even tempted.

"Not for a hundred times that," I said. "You'll have to find someone else."

"But, I want you, or at least, I want the information you're going to get," he said. "And, I'm accustomed to getting what I want."

I didn't miss the hint of steel in his voice, and I didn't like it. It was subtle, but he was threatening me.

"Sorry to have to disappoint you, but I have an ironclad rule – I don't work for two different clients on the same case." I put steel in *my* voice. The way he pursed his lips told me *he* didn't like it. At that point I really didn't care.

"You should really think carefully before you turn me down, Mr. Pennyback. People don't usually say no to me."

"There's nothing to think about," I said. "I already have a client, and as far as this case is concerned, I'm not taking on a new client. As a matter of fact, I'm not taking *any* new clients at the moment, for any cases. And, let me introduce you to the real world – if you get to know me, you'll have to get used to hearing someone say no."

He levered himself upright, glaring at me. "You'll be hearing from me again, I promise you that."

I didn't even bother standing. I just sat

there looking blankly at him. His cheeks were red and his eyes bulged. I know he wanted to say more, but since I hadn't taken his bait or looked scared after his threat, he wasn't left with much to say. He turned and walked out, his back stiff.

No doubt I would be hearing from again – or from his goons. I'd take care of that problem when it arose.

Charles Ray

9.

After Manson left, Heather came back into my office.

"What a repellent man," she said. "I felt like washing in disinfectant after he kissed my hand."

"He was a piece of work for sure," I said. I told her about his offer.

"You said no, of course."

"You know it. What do we know about this turkey?"

She held up her notebook. Naturally, she'd begun running a check on him the moment she returned to her desk. That's why I made her a partner. She didn't have to wait to be told what to do – she just knew it.

"Yes," she said. "And, boy did I find some

dirt." She flipped the book open. "He's involved in every racket in the area you can think of, from prostitution to drugs. He's been arrested a few times, but the witnesses in each case suddenly developed amnesia or disappeared, so he's never been convicted of anything."

"Did you find anything that would explain why a low level thug like Christopher Cross would be involved with someone at Manson's level, or why Manson would be interested in him?"

"I tried cross-referencing the names, but I keep coming up dry. Cross is truly just a petty con man, while Manson is into some pretty violent stuff. I don't see how their paths would ever cross." She giggled. "That's a lot of crosses in one sentence. I think I'll just refer to him as Chris from now on."

"I'm having trouble figuring out how his path crossed with Candace Kaine," I said. I giggled when she winced at the word 'crossed.' "He sounds like a real loser, and she can certainly do better. If he's tied up with a gangster like Manson, it's even worse than I thought. You keep digging. Something's fishy about this whole thing, and I want to know what it is."

"Should I focus on Chris or Manson?"

Good question. We were being paid to find

Cross. But, if he was involved with Manson, it would help to know as much about him as possible.

"Cross is our first priority, but Manson's dangerous. I suspect the two goons who attacked me at Waterfront work for him. Check him too."

Her face lit up. I'm a sucker for puzzles. Heather, on the other hand, loves to have unknown facts to dig out. In addition to having an uncanny ability to coax information from her computer – and sometimes I think she does in in ways that I'm probably best not knowing about – she has a name file containing the contact information for just about every executive assistant or office manager in the DC area. Many of them were classmates from the secretarial school she attended. I have no idea how she got to know the others, but she has a relationship with them that enables her to find out things that people think are confidential. She'd be working the phone and computer overtime on this case.

That left me to do what I do best – turn over rocks and see what scuttles out.

10.

I took off early for lunch. I drove down Fourth Street to Fort McNair, the army base that sits on the spit of land where the Potomac, the Washington Channel, and the Anacostia River all meet. The military policeman at the main gate glanced at my gray military retiree ID card and saluted me. I'd decided to eat at the officer's club, a red brick building at the north end of the grassy rectangle that forms the center of the base, not far from the spot where the plotters in Abraham Lincoln's assassination were hung – among them was Mary Surratt, at whose inn the conspirators had allegedly planned to kill the president. She was convicted along with the others and on July 7, 1865, hung from the gallows alongside the three men, becoming the first woman to be executed by the U.S. Government – but not the last. Her ghost reportedly still haunts building 20, which is located not too far from the club. It makes for some interesting conversations with some of the old timers who still drop by the club for meals now and then.

My reason for eating there, though, is more practical. The food is great, the servings are large, and the prices are low – for the Washington area – and the service is first rate. The main dining room wasn't crowded, so I was able to get a table to myself near the window, where I could look out and see the rows of brick houses for general officers that line the channel, with a view of planes taking off from National Airport in the background. They'd renamed the airport in honor of Ronald Reagan, after he left the presidency, but while he was still alive. It's now known by the cumbersome name, Ronald Reagan Washington National Airport, but it will always be just National to me. Hell, they usually wait until someone's dead to name buildings after him, but Reagan's buddies in congress began naming everything they could think of after him before the heat from his ass was off the Oval Office chairs. I didn't particularly like the guy as an actor, and he didn't impress me as much as he did some when he was president, so I couldn't understand what all the fuss was about.

I ordered braised pork chops with spicy collard greens, and a glass of unsweetened iced tea, which was in front of me in record time, along with two sweet corn muffins on a saucer, which the tiny waitress informed me were compliments of the chef. I eat there regularly, so the staff knows me. I get little perks like that from time to time.

The food, as usual, was great. I had a second glass of tea, and sat sipping it slowly as I watched the tips of the masts on sail boats gliding down the channel toward the river. It was half past one when I decided that it was time to pay a visit to Candace Kaine.

From McNair, I drove up to Maine Avenue and then crossed the National Mall on Fourteenth Street, just east of the White House. The traffic around the Mall was snarled, with tourists, busses, taxis, and a few trucks all jockeying for position in all directions. It cleared out a bit when I crossed K Street, and for the rest of the trip, I only had to deal with local traffic. In Kaine's neighborhood, except for the occasional car, the streets were pretty empty.

I drove around her block a couple times, looking for surveillance, but saw nothing. I knew it was there, though, guessing that after the first two screwed things up Manson had put someone better on the job. He was no doubt figuring that Cross would eventually come home. I was hoping that myself.

I pulled to the curb in front of the building next to hers. The same old man was sitting on the same stoop, a large bottle of malt liquor in his hand.

"Hey, young fella," he said as I got out of the car. "Mighty fine lookin' set of wheels you got there. I ain't seen one of them humpback cars in a long time."

"Is it okay if I park it here for a while?"

He looked up and down the sidewalk. "I reckon it'd be okay. But, you don't want to leave it too long. Some of these young bucks come along and see a fine green car like this, they likely to steal it for kicks. Least they'd do is steal your hubcaps."

"Can I get you to keep an eye on it?" I asked. He closed one eye, and looked up at the sky with the other. "I'll gladly pay you."

"How much you pay?"

"Five bucks?"

"Make it ten and you got a deal," he said. "What you want me to do if somebody mess with it – call up and let you know, or you want me to bust a cap in they ass?" He patted the pocket of his baggy pants.

"Uh, just yell up, and I'll run down and take care of it."

I loved the Bug, but not enough to let this old man shoot someone over it. I doubt anyone had told him that his possession of a gun in the District was illegal – or that he cared if they did. I certainly didn't want to have to explain it to the cops if he did shoot someone.

I walked over to Kaine's building and up the steps to the entrance. The door was partially ajar, making the entry buzzers little more than accessories. I pushed it open and stepped inside.

The first floor was a tight, dimly lit space with a set of mail boxes mounted on the left wall and wooden stairs on the right. Beyond the mail boxes were two doors, one in the wall next to them and one in the back wall. It was surprisingly clean, lacking the empty beer cans and litter I'd seen in so many similar buildings of its ilk in the city. Kaine's apartment was number 2B according to the address she'd put on the contract Heather had prepared for her to sign. I took the stairs, which creaked as I mounted them. On the second floor I turned left into a narrow hallway. The first door I came to had '2-B' in tarnished brass letters in the center just below a peep hole. I rapped on it.

"Just a moment," a woman's voice said from beyond the door.

The door swung inward. Candace Kaine stood there, dressed in a conservative gray pant suit. She stood aside and motioned for me to enter. The combination living-dining room was small and spartanly furnished, but everything was clean and showed care. There were toys on the sofa, and an empty glass and plate on the coffee table. A small card table with four folding chairs was in the far corner next to a low mahogany china cabinet, the most expensive looking piece of furniture in the room. On top of the cabinet were several framed photos, color shots of her and the boy, her and Cross, and Cross and the boy. The three of them looked happy in all of the pictures.

"Have you found Chris?" she asked. She had a hopeful look in her eyes.

"Not yet, but I do have a few leads," I said. "I'd like to get a bit more information from you. It might help me in my search."

"Sure, but I hope it won't take long. I'm working the night shift at the store this week, and I have to be there in an hour."

She walked over to a small sofa in the center of the living room, and pushed some of the toys aside. Her purse was on the coffee table. I sat in the matching chair across from her.

"I'll be brief. It must be hard on you,

working nights and taking care of your son."

"It was okay when Chris was here," she said. "He looked after Calvin when I worked nights. He was good at that, and the two of them had fun together. Now, though, I pay the super's mother to pick Calvin up at school and sit with him until I get home. She's an old lady with not much else to do, and the extra change she makes from babysitting makes her feel useful."

From what I'd learned about Cross, I couldn't picture him babysitting, but I still had a lot to find out about the man.

"Look, I'll get right to it. I assume you know that your boyfriend has a criminal record?"

She blushed. "Yeah, Chris has had a few brushes with the law," she said. "But, it was all small stuff. He doesn't do drugs or any really bad stuff. You have to understand, Mr. Pennyback – Chris grew up on the streets. His father took off before he was born, and his mother died when he was still a child. He was raised by his grandmother. I know he's done a little hustling, but he never hurt anyone, and he's been a good father to Calvin."

"Does the name August, or Augie, Manson mean anything to you?"

"No, I've never heard it before. No, wait, Manson – he's some kind of gangster or something, isn't he." She looked me straight in the eyes. "What does that have to do with Chris being missing?"

"I'm not sure, but my investigation has revealed that they might be involved in some kind of business deal. Manson's in organized crime, and he's also looking for Chris."

"Organized crime? You mean like the Mafia? I've heard he's a gangster of some kind, but I didn't know he was Chris wouldn't have anything to do with people like that. He's always been a loner. Are you sure about this?"

"Pretty sure," I said. I told her about the two thugs who'd attacked me, and about Manson's visit to my office.

"Oh, my God – what has Chris gotten himself into?"

"I don't know, but whatever it is, it can't be good. Have you noticed any strangers hanging around the area lately?"

"No – but, I don't know all that many people around here, and I don't pay much attention," she said.

"I'd think you would. Having a small child and all, aren't you concerned about what's in his environment?"

"You damned right I'm concerned." Her cheeks flamed crimson. "That's why I've been saving my money so we can move out of this place. I've been looking at some small houses out in Prince Georges County. I don't let Calvin go outside unless he's with me or Chris."

There was seriousness in her voice. She came across as truthful when she said she hadn't noticed any strangers. And, there was something in her voice when she mentioned Cross's name – a warmth that was unmistakable. She truly seemed to love the guy, and the body language in the pictures showed that he and the boy were close.

"Okay, but if you do see anything or anyone out of place, let me know immediately," I said. "And, tell your son's babysitter the same thing."

I left her there looking confused and clutching her purse.

11.

Things limped along slowly for the rest of the week. No leads on Cross's whereabouts, and I heard nothing more from Manson.

Saturday morning, after morning exercise and a big breakfast of steak and eggs, hash browns and biscuits, I was sitting on my back porch sipping my second cup of coffee. Sandra was at the kitchen table grading reports her students had turned in the day before. I heard the scraping of her chair and as I turned, saw her get up and head for the front of the house. She returned a few moments later with Buster in tow.

She opened the door to the porch. "You up to talking to a cop?" she asked. She had an impish smile on her beautiful face.

"Yeah, I guess so. Just make sure he's had all his shots."

"You two are really funny," Buster said. He sniffed. "Can I get a cup of that coffee?"

Sandra laughed and punched him lightly on the shoulder. "Go on out and have a seat. I'll bring your coffee."

He came onto the porch and sat in the chair next to me. Leaning back, he put his hands across his middle and took in a deep breath. "Man, you really got it made," he said. "Fresh air, a great view – wish it wasn't such a long drive into the city. I'd love to buy something out this way."

I didn't say anything. My house was in an area that had originally been farmland, but as the River Road corridor was turned more and more into havens of mega-mansions, the farmers found it more profitable to sell to developers. The former owner of my place had held out until he finally died, and his sons had put the place up for quick sale. I was in the market for a place that would give me privacy, and had a neat sum put away, and managed to put in the winning bid. I had enough acreage that my nearest neighbors were hidden from view behind the trees on either side, and was far enough back from the road that not only could I not see the traffic, but couldn't hear it, and behind me was forest that stretched all the way to the river. To find a similar deal, Buster would have to go to West Virginia – a hell of a commute for a DC cop.

"What brought you out this way on a Saturday morning?" I asked to change the subject.

Sandra came out carrying a large mug of steaming coffee, which she handed to Buster. He grabbed it in his big mitts and after blowing on it took a sip.

"Hmm, now that's a good cuppa joe," he said. He put the cup on the little wooden trestle table in front of our chairs and turned to me. "I thought you'd like to know, we got hits back on the fingerprints on the guns you took from two jamokes who tried to beat on you."

"Let me guess – they both worked for Augie Manson."

He made a growling sound. "I don't know why you even bother asking me for help," he said. "You always get the answer before the crime lab anyway. How'd you figure that one out?"

I told him about Manson's visit to my office. "Looks like the rumors of Cross being connected with Manson are right – I just can't figure out how."

"I might have the answer to that," he said. A broad smile lit up his face. "Damn, you mean I finally got the answer to something

77

before you? You must be losing your touch."

I let him have his moment. Actually, he was right – not that I really had anything to do about it - it was usually Heather who scooped the authorities by unearthing information from their own files before they could.

"So, you know what Cross was doing with or for Manson?"

"Well, it wasn't *with* or *for* – more like *to.*"

"You lost me there," I said. "What could a smalltime grifter like Cross do to a mobster like Augie Manson?"

"Look, lemme tell you the story like I heard it, okay." He took another sip of coffee. "I got this from one of my CIs – this guy works the streets in Manson's old neighborhood, keeping track of gang activity for me – anyway, he says that Manson's uncle still lives in the old hood.

I let him go on. When Buster's telling a story about one of his confidential informants, he likes to give all the background so you can judge its credibility. Or so he says. I think it's just because he likes to tell the whole story.

"Cross was working a scam in the area, and Manson's uncle was one of his marks. The old man went to his nephew and ratted

Cross out-"

"That doesn't sound like a smart move on Cross's part. Why would he mess around with a gangster's relative?"

"He might not have known," Buster said. "It was Manson's mother's brother. Doesn't matter, though – Manson's mad as hell and word is he wants the money back or Cross's head on a platter. You ask me, I think that dude wants both."

That certainly explained why Cross would want to make himself scarce. If Manson hadn't tried to hire me to find him, after hearing Buster's story, I would have put my money on Cross being somewhere under a slab of concrete, or at the bottom of the Anacostia River. If I didn't find him soon, he was likely to end up in one of those places anyway.

There was little more to say, so Buster and I just sat there watching a small herd of deer grazing at the edge of the forest, sipping our coffee and enjoying the cool morning breeze.

Charles Ray

12.

I was sitting around the house Sunday, not exactly bored, but I'd exercised, meditated, eaten breakfast, and Sandra was still grading papers, and I didn't have much to do. There wasn't much to listen to on the radio, and the case was on my mind. So, I told Sandra I was going for a drive. She barely looked up from the stack of papers spread out on the coffee table as I walked past. She might have grunted something, but I didn't really hear it.

Buster had given me Manson's uncle's address. It was in The Gregory Estates apartments in Prince Georges County, Maryland, a bunch of low cost apartments built in the late 1940s. The availability of affordable housing outside the District had attracted a mass migration of black families into an area that had been all-white, but that was now over 90 percent black. Both sides of

Manson's family had come from there, and it was where he had grown up. Seat Pleasant's crime rate is higher than the national average, which explains in part Manson's choice of career. Unlike many from his neighborhood, though, he'd been smart enough to dodge the law for most of his teen years, and had associated himself with key organized crime figures in the District as a young man. He'd now risen high in the organization, basically in control of most of the organized crime activity in the area around Seat Pleasant, and most of the Southeast and Northeast areas of the District. According to Buster's sources, the word on the street was that Manson was positioning himself to take over the entire region. He was not a man whose bad graces you wanted to be in.

Manson's uncle lived in a two-story brick building just off Central Avenue and south of the football stadium where the Washington team played its home games. The buildings were relatively well maintained, and sat in orderly rows on ground elevated from the street, with gnarled hardwood trees in back and brownish-green swaths of grass around them. There were eight buildings in his complex, surrounded by a four-foot-high chain link fence. The gate in the center of the fence was unlocked, but as I parked on the street in the first empty space I found and got out of my Volkswagen, I had the feeling that dozens of pairs of eyes were on me from the blank windows of the nearby buildings.

At that hour on Sunday morning there were few people on the streets. Most would be in church, sleeping off a Saturday night drunk, or watching the early sports matches on TV.

The gate squeaked loudly as I pushed it open. As I approached the building, the second from the right, the dark windows with their white frames and shutters, increased the feeling that I was being watched.

Unlike Candace Kaine's apartment, with its unsecured front door, the front doors of this building were heavy wood and locked, with a bank of buttons at the side. You had to buzz the person you were visiting and wait for them to push a button in their apartment that opened the door. I scanned the bank for Manson's uncle – Seymour Wilson. I found S. Wilson in the second row – apartment 2G. I pressed the scuffed white button beneath his name.

"Yeah, who is it?" A raspy, but tinny voice came from the grate at the top of the bank of buttons.

I leaned forward, my mouth a few inches from the grate that also doubled as a mike. "Mr. Wilson, Mr. Seymour Wilson? My name is Al Pennyback. I'm a private investigator, and I'm working on a case that I think you could help me with."

"What kinda case you talkin' 'bout?"

"I'd really rather discuss that in a more . . . private environment," I said. "It's a rather sensitive matter."

"What it got to do with me?"

"I think you might be acquainted with one of the principal figures in my case," I said. "You're not in any kind of trouble, I assure you. I just need some background information on this person."

There was a long pause. I could hear him mumbling, but couldn't make out what he was saying. "Okay, come on up," he said finally.

There was a buzz and click from the door. I quickly pushed it opened and entered the lobby. It was wide, with a stairwell on the left and mailboxes on the right, and two apartment doors on either side. I took the stairs to the second floor. Wilson's apartment was the first on the left. I walked to his door and rang the bell.

"Lemme see your ID in front of the peephole," his voice said from behind the door.

I held my PI card up to the brass-rimmed hole. After a few seconds I heard a chain rattle and the 'snick' of locks, and the door opened.

Seymour Wilson was a short, rotund man, bald on top, with slicked down hair on the sides and back of his round skull. His skin was the color of caramel, but with dark moles on his face like raisins. His eyes were blood shot and watery. As I entered the apartment, I saw the half empty bottle of cheap scotch on a glass and metal coffee table, which explained the eyes. The living room was neat, except for the greasy box next to the liquor bottle, which contained a half-eaten pizza. He motioned me to the black leather sofa.

"Thanks for agreeing to talk to me," I said. "I'll try not to take too much of your time."

I sat on the end of the sofa. The Sunday edition of the *Washington Post* took up the other end. He swept it to the floor, scattering the sections all over, and sat, turned so he could face me. His expression was wary.

"Now, what you want to talk about?"

"Do you know a man by the name of Christopher Cross?" I asked.

His fleshy lips turned down in a frown, and the look of wariness deepened.

"Why you want to know?"

"I'll take that as a yes," I said. "In what capacity are you acquainted with Mr. Cross?"

His brows wrinkled in confusion. Then, he smiled crookedly. It wasn't at all a friendly smile. "Oh, you mean, how I know him? You tell me why you want to know, and maybe I tell you how come I know him. You a friend of his?"

"No, I've never met the man," I said. "I was hired to find him. I'm talking to everyone who might know him. Now, will you answer my question?"

"Sure, I tell you how I know that little fuck. He done took me for a lotta money is how I know him. You find him you tell him I wants my money back. He don't pay up, my nephew gone bust him up good. You tell him that."

"How did he get money from you?"

His cheeks darkened. I could guess that he'd been scammed because he was greedy and had fallen for a get-rich-quick scheme of some sort, and was now embarrassed about it. But, I don't like to make too many assumptions in one month, so I waited for him to answer. He blinked and looked at me, his lips quivering.

"He done told me that he had this deal where I could buy these machines to put in the airport and bus station what let people get on the Internet," he said. "They cost ten thousand each, and I done signed up for ten. I give that little shit cash up front."

"Did the machines get delivered?"

"Yeah, they did, but he didn't tell me I had to apply for come kinda license 'fore I could put 'em in the airport or over to the bus terminal. That gone cost me another couple thousand bucks. Then I find out most I can make is 'bout five or ten bucks a month for each machine. At that rate it take me a hundred years to make my money back. When I look for him to get my money back, the number he give me turn out to be phony. So now I'm stuck with ten pieces of junk, and ain't no money comin' in at all, 'cause I couldn't get permission to put 'em in."

I almost felt sorry for him – just almost. He fell for the scheme because of greed, and stupidity. He should have done his homework *before* putting up the money. That didn't excuse Cross, though. I could see why Manson was pissed at him. Still, I owed loyalty to my client. She wanted the little shit back, and it was my job to find him and deliver – and, I was sure she wanted him alive and in one piece.

"I'm sorry for your loss, Mr. Wilson," I said. "I take it you have no idea where Cross is right now?"

"Naw, 'cause if I did, I'd tell my nephew – Augie Manson – and, he'd send some of his boys over and bust that little fuck's legs after they got my money back from him."

I looked confused. No sense letting him know that I knew who and what his nephew was.

"Is your nephew with the police?"

"With the po-lice?" He laughed and slapped his knees. "Now, that is really funny. Naw, Augie ain't with no po-lice. He . . . what you call it . . . an independent businessman." He seemed to find that even funnier. He laughed until tears rolled from the corner of his eyes.

I took a business card from my wallet. "Well, if you should happen to get a lead on Cross's whereabouts, I'd appreciate if you'd give me a call."

He took the card and squinted at it before putting it on the table next to the pizza box. "Sure, I do that. Right after I call Augie. You got any more questions?"

I didn't, so I thanked him for his time and left. I wasn't any closer to finding Christopher Cross, but I now knew more about him and the trouble he was in. He'd probably been smart to run. If Manson got his hands on him, he'd be toast. I couldn't let that happen. He still wouldn't win my citizen of the year award, but I knew that if I didn't find him before Manson did, he'd be fertilizing some vacant lot somewhere. That would let my client down, and I don't like letting people down. Besides, I'd developed an even more intense dislike for Augie Manson. It would give me great pleasure to thwart his plans.

If only I could figure out how to do it.

Charles Ray

13.

After returning home, I made a few sketchy notes about my visit to Seymour Wilson – not a lot of clues, but a good bit background information. One thing I knew for sure. Cross was way up a creek in a leaky boat.

When I got to the office on Monday morning, I tore the page from my notebook and gave it to Heather to add to the case file. She keeps a complete file of every case we do. On the one hand, she says the files are useful at the end of the year when we do taxes, because she keeps a meticulous list of all expenses and fees. On the other, she keeps bugging me to consider writing a book about my adventures as a PI – and I keep ignoring her. I don't like writing. I mean, I'm okay when it comes to jotting down notes of an interview, or when I'm on a stakeout, but writing hundreds of pages describing what I do appeals to me about as much as getting a colonoscopy – without anesthetic.

While Heather did whatever it is she does with her computer, I pulled out a fresh notebook and sat there staring at the blank pages trying to put some structure to the case which was going nowhere.

At the top of the page I wrote Christopher Cross's name. Then, starting with Candace Kaine, I wrote every name I'd come across that seemed associated with Cross. Then, I wrote the reason he had for disappearing – or what I thought the reason was. It was a scanty list:

Christopher Cross (missing)

Candace Kaine (girlfriend? Common law wife?)

August 'Augie' Manson (looking for Cross)

Seymour Wilson (Manson's uncle, scammed by Cross)

Cross skipped town after running scam on Wilson

Manson out to find Cross (to do what?)

Not a lot to go on. In fact, nothing at all to go on. I had a lot of work to do. I'd tried meditating, but that hadn't given me any brilliant flashes of insight. Maybe talking about it would help. I took my notebook and walked out to Heather's domain.

She was just getting off the phone. Little worry lines were on her forehead.

"What's up?" I asked.

"I just got off the phone with a guy I know in the Washington Passport Office," she said. "Christopher Cross applied for a passport last week."

The little rat was planning to leave the country. That might slow Manson down a little, but it wouldn't help me either. My reach doesn't extend much beyond the Washington metro area.

"That can't be good. If he leaves the country we'll never find him – but, then again, it'll be harder for Augie Manson to find him, too."

"He's not going anywhere yet," she said. "My friend said he just put in a routine application instead of asking for expedited processing. With their current workload, his passport won't be issued for six to eight weeks."

I hired Heather right out of secretarial school when I started working as a PI because I needed someone to do the paperwork. She turned out to also be a whiz with a computer, which made her even more valuable as an assistant. But, she's also pretty good at investigating – I hadn't thought to check and see if Cross had applied for a passport. I'd been teaching her investigation techniques, but she was doing a pretty good job on her own. Then, a stray thought crawled up from the basement of my brain and slapped the back of my head.

"Hey," I said. "If he applied for a passport, he had to give a mailing address."

"Way ahead of you on that, boss. Unfortunately, it's one of those mail drop places. Good news, though, it's not far from here – over near N Street and Third, not far from the Navy Yard."

She wrote the address on one of those yellow Post-it™ notes and handed it to me.

"I guess I should go over there and see if he gave this place an address."

I was guessing he either hadn't, or had given a phony address. That's what I would have done. But, a slim lead was better than no lead at all. Heather usually has a little pixie smile when she ferrets out new information, but she was still frowning. I gave her the right eyebrow raised look that said, 'spill it.'

"I, uh, found out more about this Manson character," she said. "And, none of it is good."

Straddling the chair near her desk, I propped my elbows on the back and rested my chin on my interlaced fingers. "What could be worse than what we already know?"

"Remember I said he's never been convicted of anything because the witnesses got amnesia?" I nodded. "Well, a couple of witnesses completely disappeared."

"Disappeared – as in probably murdered?"

"Yes, but since no bodies were ever found, they were never able to charge him with anything. No one has reported the missing people, leaving the police with nothing to go on."

I made 'tsking' sounds. "Our Mr. Manson is a bad boy," I said. "I might just have to have an attitude adjustment session with him."

"You can't be thinking of going up against him," she said. Her pupils were two blue marbles encircled by milky whiteness. "He has some really nasty people working for him."

"I know, I met two of them, remember? Don't worry, though. If I decide to confront him, it'll be on my terms. Right now, I think I'll pop over to the mail box place and see if I can get a lead on Cross."

I got up, tucked my notebook into my belt, and went down to the parking lot. I normally like to use the subway system to get around, but the temperature and humidity were rising, and I didn't want to have to try and get information from someone while I was sweating like a sewer worker. I had to turn the Bug's a/c on almost as soon as I got in, because the inside felt like a sweat box. Sandra had suggested I get it serviced in March, and it was a good thing, because it was beginning to look like it would get a lot of use.

The mail box place was a little hole in the wall operation in the center of the block, sandwiched between a fast food joint and a drugstore. I didn't find an empty parking space in that block, but caught a van pulling out in the next, and luckily he'd left twenty minutes on the meter. Despite the air conditioning in my car, I was still sweating by the time I got back to the shop.

It was as tiny inside as it looked from outside. A counter set back midway that ran the width of the room, behind which were rows of medium sized mail boxes. A table on the left had pamphlets, mailing labels, envelopes, and pens, and on the right were ten plastic chairs for waiting customers. They were all empty.

A cute girl with smooth *café au lait* skin and straightened black hair streaked with red stood behind the counter. She smiled at me and pulled her shoulders back; thrusting her small pointed breasts against the thin cotton blouse she wore.

"Can I help you?" she asked.

I ignored her flirting.

"I certainly hope so," I said. "I'm trying to track down one of your customers.

I showed her my ID. Her smile faded. I then pulled out the photo strip and laid it on the counter, putting a finger next to Cross's image.

"Have you ever seen this guy before?"

She peered down at the photos, and shook her head.

"I don't know. He looks kinda familiar, but we get lots of people in here. I couldn't possibly remember every one of them."

"Okay," I said. "It was a long shot. The customer I'm interested in is Christopher Cross. I'm trying to locate him."

"I'm not supposed to divulge a customer's personal information," she said. "It's against company policy."

I leaned over the counter until my face was only inches from hers, and gave her my thousand-watt smile. She blushed. "I don't want you to get into any trouble," I said in a low, hopefully seductive, voice. "But, it's really important that I find this guy. He's owed some money, and if I can't find him it'll just go to the government."

I don't know if it was my animal magnetism, or the idea that the government stood to get some poor schmuck's money, but she breathed deeply. "Okay, I suppose I could look it up for you. What did you say his name was again?"

I told her. She went to the side and opened the top drawer of a three-drawer cabinet that sat at the end of the counter. She flipped through folders until she found what she was looking for. Opening the manila folder, which I could see only contained a single sheet, she looked at it with a puzzled frown on her face.

"Problem?" I asked.

"Yeah, sort of," she said. "There's no home address on the application form."

"Is there a credit card number or bank reference?"

"No, the customer paid in cash according to this."

Damn, I thought, another dead end. I shrugged. "Well, thanks for trying. It was worth a shot."

I turned to go.

"Hey, wait a minute," she said. "I just

remembered something." I turned back. "I remember the guy now. A little dude, not a big hunk of dark meat like you." She smiled broadly at me, leaning forward again and breathing deeply, causing her breasts to jiggle slightly. "He came in a while back and rented a box. Paid for the first two months in cash."

"Did he drive or come in a cab – did you see?"

"No, he walked. I remember, 'cause he was sweating like you when you come in, and there were no cars parked in front. He didn't come far, though, 'cause he wasn't sweating all that much."

"So, you think he lives around here somewhere?"

"There's a coupla flop houses in the neighborhood," she said. "But, I don't see this dude living in one. He had a wad of bills on him that would choke an elephant."

No help there at all, really. But, I'd check the flop houses out just to be sure. She looked disappointed when I thanked her and turned to leave. I have no idea what she was thinking was going to happen.

Charles Ray

14.

I spent most of the afternoon checking out the flop houses and tenements in the area around the mail store – and came up empty.

It was a quarter to five when I got back to the office. Candace Kaine, a wild look in her eyes, got out of a cab just as I got out of my car. She ran over to me and grabbed the front of my shirt.

"They took him," she said. Tears ran down her face. "They took him. You got to get him back."

I placed my hands on her shoulders. She was trembling. "Slow down," I said. "Who took who? What are you talking about?"

"C-Calvin, my baby - somebody took him."

I didn't think it was a good idea to try and calm her down and have a conversation in the parking lot, so I guided her up the rickety stairs, into the office, and onto the chair in front of Heather's desk. Heather took one look at her face and immediately poured her a cup of fragrant tea, insisting that she drink some before answering anymore of my questions.

"Okay," I said when she looked calmer. "Start from the beginning, and tell us what happened."

She took a deep breath. "I got off work early today, so I thought I'd pick Calvin up from school. I called Ms. Johnson – the super's mother – and told her so she wouldn't have to walk all that way. When I got to the school, they said Calvin's dad had already picked him up. You can imagine how that made me feel – I thought Chris had come back. So, I rushed home. But, they weren't there. All I found was this note."

She reached into her purse and withdrew a folded sheet of construction paper of the kind kids use in school for art projects. She unfolded it and handed it to me. The note, written in black crayon, was blunt and to the point:

> You want your brat back, give up Cross.
> I'll contact you in 24 hrs and tell you what to do.

That was it – no ID, and I'd be willing to

bet there'd be no fingerprints on the paper. It had to be Manson, though.

"What do I do?" she asked. Tears streamed down her cheeks.

"I think I know who is behind this," I said. "For now, though, you should go home and wait for them to call."

"You think it's a good idea to send her back there by herself?" Heather asked.

"I'll be okay," she said. "And, I need to be there when whoever took Calvin calls."

Heather had a point, but I wasn't comfortable sending her, and I had something that had to be done. Then, I thought of Buster.

"I have a friend who works Metro PD," I said. "I'll give him a call and have him keep an eye on your place."

Her eyes went wide. "You sure that's a good idea? If whoever took my boy sees police around – who knows what they might do."

"Don't worry. Buster can be discrete. He knows the drill in cases like this."

She still looked skeptical – and, I suppose I couldn't really blame her – but, she finally agreed. I called Buster, and without telling him about the boy's kidnapping, asked if he'd have someone keep an eye on her building, but not let it be known that cops were watching. He must have detected something in my voice.

"What's going on, Al?" he asked.

"Can't tell you right now, bro, but I'm concerned that my client might be in a bit of trouble. Just want an eye kept on her for a few hours."

"Okay, in that case, I'll do it myself. I don't work the streets in that neighborhood, so nobody's likely to know I'm a cop."

When he wanted to, Buster could look like a tough street thug – the kind you didn't want to mess with. Candace Kaine would be safe with him on guard. I gave him Kaine's address, thanked him and hung up.

"You're good to go," I told her. "I'll replace my friend Buster as soon as I take care of a little business."

After she left, Heather planted her tiny frame in front of me, her hands on her hips and a defiant look on her face.

"Just what is this business that's so important?" she asked in a no-nonsense voice. "You're not planning to do something dangerous and stupid, are you?"

The woman reads me like a comic book

with mostly pictures. No point trying to keep it from her. "I plan to pay Mr. Manson a visit," I said. "I think he's behind this, and if he is, I want to let him know that I don't think much of people who involve kids in junk like this."

"Just what I thought," she said. She made a snorting sound. "Dangerous *and* stupid, and I'll bet there's no chance of me talking you out of it, is there?"

"You win that bet, kid. I'll call you when I'm on my way to Kaine's apartment."

15.

Based on the information Buster had given me, August Manson's operations were run out of a three-story red brick building on L Street north of Union Station, and not far from the main bus terminal. The area was like many areas near transportation terminals – seedy and run down, with many abandoned and boarded up buildings and weed and trash strewn lots, some surrounded by rusted chain link fences with more breaks than link. When the city cleaned up the Fourteenth Street corridor, a lot of the drug dealers and hookers moved their operations northeast to this area.

It was nearly seven when I turned right off North Capitol Street onto L, and business was already booming. A couple of hookers, one of whom looked like a high school student despite the makeup and miniskirt that barely covered her crotch, waved at my

Volkswagen as I drove past, and then gave me the middle finger 'up yours' sign when I didn't even slow down. A little past them was a hulking figure in a hoodie standing on the corner trying to look casual. He was either their pimp or a dealer – or both. He glared at me as I drove past him. I was beginning to have second thoughts about coming to what was a more dangerous war zone than most I'd encountered when I was working special operations in the army. Despite my skin color, I was as out of place as a white government worker from the suburbs. And, unlike him, I wasn't looking to score anything, which made me the enemy. The only advantage, or at least I hoped the only advantage, was that my Volkswagen wasn't likely to interest any of the carjackers who might be lurking in the shadows on the poorly lit sidewalks waiting for an expensive set of wheels to boost.

Manson's building wasn't hard to spot. It was the only one with a clean sidewalk in front and a neat parking area to one side that held several expensive looking cars. I also noticed that the drug dealers and whores all gave it a wide berth. It was as if there was an invisible force field around it. Even the parking lot, with all the flashy cars, didn't seem to be guarded. It was well lit, unlike all the other lots, and even the sidewalks, where every third or fourth street lamp had been broken. There were four big floodlights, one at each corner, aimed inward. I imagine someone inside the building looked out occasionally to make sure nothing had breached the exclusion zone.

I didn't want to draw attention by entering the parking lot, so I parked on the street, but near enough that it was clear I was headed to the big building. There were four or five other cars on the street as well. I got out and made a production of locking the doors before walking up to the single wooden door in the front of the structure. It was at the right side of the front wall with one window to its right and a row of five to the left. The windows were covered inside with some dark material that turned them into mirrors reflecting the dingy buildings across the street. There was a small brass plate on the door – 'Private Club – Members Only.' I pushed against it. It swung inward. I stepped in.

I found myself in a space the size of a broom closet, but with dark fabric instead of wood for walls. It was lit by a single bulb in a fixture in the ceiling. There was a table to my right, behind which sat a thin, balding man with a gold tooth that flashed when he smiled up at me. To my front, standing in front of a slit in the fabric, was a mean looking bald dude wearing a black t-shirt that looked like it had been painted on the muscles of his chest and arms. Both of them eyed me through the thin slits of half-closed eyes, but I was pretty sure they were checking for a couple of things – that I wasn't packing, and that I wasn't a cop. People in neighborhoods like this have a sixth sense for both. The one keeps you alive, and the other keeps you out of the slammer. I must have passed muster. The thin guy smiled at me, and Muscles just looked at me as if was now measuring my ability to use my hands. Little did he know that I was also pretty good with my feet. I hoped I wouldn't have to demonstrate my ability.

"Hello," the thin guy said. "Haven't seen you in here before. Are you a member?"

He didn't score too high in the brains department. If he hadn't seen me before, he couldn't possibly think I was a member. I'd lay even money that despite his apparent lack of intelligence, he remembered everyone who passed through the door.

Muscles was looking me up and down. He had two inches and probably twenty pounds on me, and one of his hands made two of mine – which is saying something, because at six-one and two hundred, I'm no featherweight.

I figured the place for an unlicensed drinking establishment or an illegal gambling club. It was unlikely that they had too many people stumble in accidentally. I decided to play along.

"No, I've never been here before, but a friend of mine recommended it. How do I become a member?"

Gold tooth smiled up at me. The tooth bounced the light from the overhead bulb in my eyes like the flash from a camera.

"Membership cost fifty dollah," he said. "Cash only. We don't take plastic."

An illegal gambling club, then. Manson was into everything. I took out my wallet and extracted two twenties and a ten and placed them on the table. Gold tooth's slender brown hand moved swiftly and the bills disappeared. He inclined his head toward Muscles who stepped aside. I didn't bother asking for a receipt or membership card. My sense was they didn't like leaving a paper trail, and that the membership dues were fifty dollars a visit. I only planned this one visit, and I could eat this expense. I don't like charging clients for expenses without receipts to back them up.

I brushed past Muscles and stepped through the slit in what I could see were thick maroon drapes that when closed had blocked the din from inside the large room which was filled with people sitting in groups at tables scattered around – some playing various forms of poker, a few playing blackjack, and two old guys in the corner playing dominos Six guys in overalls stood at the bar that dominated the back wall. On a stage at the right a bored looking Asian girl with small naked breasts that barely moved as she swung her hips and thrust her pelvis to the beat of an unrecognizable tune coming from two large speakers at either side of the stage. Several men, some in suits, some in workers' togs, stood or sat along the front of the stage, throwing crumpled banknotes at her feet. Their hooting and cheering vied with the music and the din of conversation from the gamblers for space in my ears, setting up a vibration in my head. The room was dimly lit, except for the one floodlight that shone on the stripper.

I stood there a few minutes to let my eyes adjust to the dimness and the din. My ears were the first to adjust. The wavering cloud of blue smoke from the cigars and cigarettes that most of the customers were puffing on made it hard to see clearly. But, slowly, things started to resolve themselves. The competing smells in the smoke were harder to adapt to, and the stinging sensation and acrid scent in my nose told me that not everyone was smoking tobacco.

As I looked around, trying to decide whether to move to the bar or sit at one of the three empty tables, a large breasted woman with braided hair, jet black and shiny and streaked with bright red, walked up to me. She had skin the color of caramel, a high forehead, and a long neck that, along with the sarong she wore wrapped tightly around her breasts and ample hips, made her look like the picture of an Ethiopian princess I'd seen at a photo exhibit Sandra and I had attended one weekend.

"Can I get you a drink, mister?" she asked, looking at one of the empty tables.

The hopeful look in her almond eyes said she'd marked me as a generous tipper. I hated to disappoint her, but I had business to attend to. I didn't need the distraction.

"No," I said. "I think I'll sit at the bar." She looked crestfallen. I took a five from my wallet and tucked it into the top of her sarong, copping a feel of the top of her breast. "Maybe next time."

She smiled broadly and put her hand over mine, pressing it into the soft swell. "You know where to find me, hon," she said. She turned and walked away, her hips swinging seductively.

I walked to the end of the bar farthest from the stage and straddled the padded stool, leaning my elbows on the Formica top. The bartender, a light-skinned man with a bad case of acne, came over.

"What can I get you, friend?"

A clear mind is essential when you're in enemy territory, but I needed to blend in. "Vodka tonic," I said.

"Which vodka you prefer?"

"Make it stoli."

"Single or double?"

"Single, please," I said. They probably watered the drinks, but there was no sense taking chances.

He went back to the center and took a bottle of Stolichnaya from the shelf and filled a shot glass. He poured the clear liquid into a tumbler and then added tonic from the tap, and then added two ice cubes and a twist of lime. He brought it back and placed it in front of me.

"You want to run a tab?" he asked.

"No, how much do I owe you?"

"That'll be five bucks."

That was pretty cheap for a mixed drink – even a watered down one.

I put a ten spot on the counter, which he quickly whisked away. He went to the register under the bar and then returned with five ones which he put on the bar, keeping his hand near them. I pulled three ones from the stack and nodded. He smiled as he made the two remaining bills disappear.

I took a sip of the vodka. He hadn't watered it, and the fiery liquor stung my throat as it slid down. Putting the glass on the bar, I spun around on the stool and began a more careful scan of the place. There was no sign of Augie Manson, but I noticed several of the card players at my end of the bar were paying more attention to me than the cards in their hands.

After a while, I noticed that the guys watching me were also looking at a door in the wall that I hadn't seen before. I figured Manson was behind that door. Turning back to the bar, I kept my back to it, so my watchers wouldn't know what I knew. That left me with the problem, though, of how to get to the man.

He solved the problem for me.

For such a big man, Manson could move awful quietly. I didn't even sense him coming up behind me until he was close enough to touch me.

"Well, Mr. Pennyback," his gravelly voice echoed in my ear. "I see you've come to visit. You change your mind about my offer?"

I turned slowly to face him. Sitting on the

stool, I was still taller. But, with no telling how many of his goons in the place, he had me outnumbered.

"No, I was just curious to see where you hang out."

He blinked.

"You find Cross yet?"

"No, but I have a counteroffer for you," I said. "When I find him, if I can get your uncle's money, will you back off?"

He blinked twice.

"What do you know about my uncle?"

"I'm a private detective, remember. It's my job to find out things. Didn't you think I'd look into why you're so interested in finding a penny ante grifter like Cross?"

His eyes did a little dance from side to side.

"Uh, if you can get the money back," he said, looking at my feet. "I, uh, suppose I wouldn't need to talk to the little shit. You sure you ain't found him?"

He lied. His shifty eyes and refusal to meet my gaze told me so. I don't particularly like being lied to.

"Why don't I believe that you still don't

want to rough him up a little?" I asked him.

Now he looked me in the eye. An angry scowl made his unattractive face even uglier.

"You calling me a liar?"

He hadn't raised his voice, but it was loud enough to be heard at the nearby tables, where all conversations had stopped, and the two of us were the center of attention.

"Look, if someone had gypped a relative of mine out of that much money, I'd be pretty pissed too," I said. "So, I can understand you wanting to take a chunk out of Cross's ass. In fact, I figure you'd do just about anything to put a little hurt on him – am I wrong in that assumption?"

A mix of emotions flickered on his face – anger, confusion, surprise, uncertainty. Then, his expression hardened.

"A man in my business can't afford to let anyone get away with stuff like this."

That was about as close as he was going to get to admitting that he had more in mind for Cross. It was good enough for me to try one more piece of bait in the water.

"I get it," I said. "But, what I don't agree with is involving innocents in the fight – especially kids."

His eyes widened, only for an instance, but long enough for me to know one of the things I'd come to learn.

"What's that supposed to mean?"

He tried for a neutral expression, but his eyes wouldn't stay still.

"I think you know," I said. I stood and brushed past him, heading for the exit.

All the way to the curtain I felt an itch between my shoulder blades, but I didn't look back. The itchy feeling didn't go away until I was outside and sitting behind the wheel of my car.

Now, I had to find where they were holding the boy. I'd dropped the bait. I felt pretty confident that Manson would bite.

16.

I didn't figure Manson would go himself. But, he'd be curious about the extent of my knowledge of the kidnapping, so he'd probably send someone to check on things. I relied on the fact that none of them would recognize my green Volkswagen – maybe assuming it belonged to one of their yuppie customers – so I sat hunched in the seat.

The wait wasn't long.

Two figures in dark shirts and pants, one with a ball cap pulled down over his face and the other wearing a hoodie, exited the building and walked briskly to the parking lot. A few minutes later a metallic blue and white Ford Fairlane that shuddered as it moved, indicating that the old model had been reconditioned and outfitted with a new more powerful engine, nosed into the street, turned right and zipped past me. I had my windows down to let air in, and the noise of the Ford's engine bounced around inside my head for several seconds. I let them get to the corner before moving away from the curb and following.

The Fairlane, with its square back and bright color scheme, was easy to follow, so I hung back about six car lengths. I didn't notice the lights behind me until I'd made a third turn behind the Fairlane. The follower was being followed. I couldn't make out the type of vehicle, just the two circles of light that stayed four car lengths or so back, turning when I did. When I did a mental inventory, I realized that the lights had been there since I left Manson's place.

The car I was following went up North Capitol Street and then right on R Street. At U.S. Route 1, it turned left and went north until it reached the outskirts of Hyattsville, where it turned right onto an unmarked two lane road that was lined by small bungalows on each side. When I saw the brake lights flash, I pulled over and waited. Up ahead, the car pulled left into a driveway to a small one-story white house with a dark roof and dark trim. The street light in front of the house was out, leaving the small yard in deep shadow. I could see the two men get out of the car and enter the house. A sliver of light flashed as they went through the front door, but the place must have had heavy curtains, for no light showed in any of the windows.

I got out of the car and locked the doors. Looking back down the street, I saw no sign of the car that had been following me. Nor were there any pedestrians or other vehicles in sight. I walked quickly across the street and made my way between two houses. There was a dirt lane behind the houses, with garbage cans behind some. The neighborhood was quiet, except for the hum of noise from a TV set in the house to my right. I walked slowly toward the right, stopping every few steps and looking around. When I was two houses away from the house the men had entered, a cat jumped from the top of a garbage can and made a yowling noise as it scurried off into the darkness. I froze in place, every sense alert for anyone who might have heard the animal, but it remained quiet.

When I reached the corner of the last house, I crouched behind another garbage can and peered around it to assess the situation.

Many of the street lights in front of the houses were out, but there were no lights in the service alley behind them. The buildings cast long shadows, black rectangles broken by six-foot wide strips of gray where the weak light from the few functioning lamps cast a glow. I would have to cross that gray strip to reach the house.

I crouched there, steadying my breathing and listening for any sound that might indicate I'd been spotted. Just as I started to rise and make a dash for the shadow behind the house, I saw a dark figure dart from behind the house to the left, and stop near the garbage can there. I couldn't make out the person's face, but it looked like a small man from the way the figure ran. He rose and started across the lane just as I stepped from behind the can.

We both entered the lighted area at the same time. That's when he saw me. His mouth opened in a round, dark shape and his eyes were like two white marbles with black circles as he stared at me.

"Who the fuck are you?" Christopher Cross asked in a hoarse whisper.

17.

I grabbed him by the shoulders and pulled him back into the shadows. He tried pulling away, but I had too many pounds on him. I pushed him down to a crouching position and knelt next to him.

"My name is Al Pennyback," I whispered. "I'm a private detective. Your girlfriend hired me to find you. Now, you mind telling me what you're doing here?"

In the dim light I could see the fear in his eyes. "How I know you don't work for Augie Manson?" he asked with a quavering voice.

"Because, if I did, I'd have knocked you

out and stuffed you in the trunk of my car. Or maybe just busted your head and taken you to Rock Creek Park for the animals to eat. I told you, your girlfriend Candace hired me to find you. Why'd you run out on her and her kid like that?"

He looked confused as he processed what I'd said. Finally, he sighed and looked down at his feet.

"Yeah, I know that was a shitty thing to do," he said. "But, I was afraid if I went to the apartment, Manson or one of the dudes workin' for him might see me, and they'd try to use Candy to get to me."

"Looks like they're doing that anyway," I said. "Why on earth would you run a scam on a mobster's relative?"

"Hell, I didn't know that old dude was kin to Augie Manson. You think I'd have done that had I known? I ain't crazy. 'Sides, he came to me. He heard about the vending machine project and wanted a piece of it."

"Why didn't you just give him his money back?"

"I was gone do that," he said. "But, when I was on my way to his house, a bro of mine said Manson was lookin' for me. Man, I panicked. Manson don't play. That dude's likely to have me fed to a pack of stray dogs or something."

"Okay, I guess I can see that. So, what are you doing here?"

Anger flashed across his face. "I heard that bastard done took my boy. I borrowed a car from a dude I know, and come here to get him back."

I couldn't help it. The guy probably weighed one-fifty, fully clothed and soaking wet, and there had to be at least three guys in that house, probably armed, but he had a determined look on his face. I reassessed my opinion of him. He'd done what I would have done – keep away from loved ones to try and keep them out of danger, but when danger finds them, come back and try to help. There wasn't jack he could do, but I gave him credit for wanting.

"How did you plan to do that?" I asked.

"Uh, well, I hadn't really thought it out that far," he said. "Why you here?"

"Same reason," I said. "When Candy told me someone had snatched the boy, and the note mentioned trading him for you, I knew it had to be Manson. I went to his place tonight to bait him, and he bit. I think he worried that I might have located where he was holding the kid, and sent his two gunsels to check on it – I followed them and, *voila*, here we are."

"So, what's your plan to get my boy back?"

"Uh, I hadn't actually thought it out completely myself," I said. "But, with you here, I have an idea."

I told him what I had in mind. I gave him more credit. He looked scared at what I asked him to do, but agreed anyway, even though if things went wrong we could both get our asses shot off.

18.

We walked quickly through the patch of light and hugged the rear corner of the house, staying in its shadow. When I was satisfied we were still undetected, I had Cross follow me as we worked our way along the wall to the front. In the dim light, he had an expression of uncertainty on his face, and worry in his eyes. I understood his anxiety. I was asking him to walk willingly back into the lion's den.

At the front of the house, we stopped. I peered around the corner. The car I'd been following still sat in the driveway. The front lawn was only dimly illuminated because the street light in front of the house was out, and the light over the front door wasn't turned on. That would help my plan.

I motioned for Cross to follow me as I stepped around the corner. As we passed a window I could hear a muffled sound from inside. I couldn't make out whether it was someone in the room talking or a television. The curtains were drawn tightly drawn. I couldn't even tell if there was a light on in the room. At the door I stopped and took stock of the area. There was a concrete pad in front of the door which was solid wood with a small arched glassed in opening at the top. The concrete pad extended a foot past the door on either side. I looked down and saw that the door knob was on the right, so I moved to the right side of the door and flattened myself against the wall.

"Okay," I whispered. "Ring the bell"

"You sure there ain't another way we can do this?" he asked with a plaintive note.

"Look, don't get cold feet on me now. If you do like I told you everything will be fine."

I tried to put as much conviction as possible into my voice. There *was* a chance that if whoever came to the door moved fast enough, or if I didn't time my move just right, he could suffer some damage. I didn't think they'd want to do anything to him before consulting with their boss though. Sure, it was a bit of a long shot, but I was certain that they were holding Calvin Kaine in that house, and I was determined to get him out.

"Okay, I'll do it, but you get that bastard

fast and I'll get Calvin."

He was as determined as I was to get his son back. So determined, he seemed to have forgotten that there were three guys in the house. Fortunately, his anger and determination gave him the grit he needed to go through with the plan. He reached up and pressed the doorbell button. I could hear discordant chimes from somewhere inside the house. When I saw the door knob start to rotate, I tensed.

The door swung inward, and a shadow fell over Cross and the concrete pad.

"What you wa– Damn, Cross, what the hell you doin' here? Augie been lookin' all over for you."

Cross's mouth opened and closed several times. His forehead was shiny with sweat, and it wasn't all from the heat. I was afraid he'd blow it, but he swallowed, his Adam's apple bobbing up and down, and took a deep breath.

"I c-come to g-get my boy," he said. Then, just as I'd told him to do, he took a step backwards.

"How you know we -, shit, first thing you gone do is talk to Augie," the guy in the doorway said. "You come on in while I call him."

As I'd anticipated, these guys would need orders and they'd want to hold Cross until those orders came. The man in the doorway stepped forward, reaching for the front of Cross's shirt.

He never saw my fist coming. I slammed a right into his temple, stunning him. His mouth opened, and his eyes squeezed shut, but before he could make a sound beyond a slight wheezing, I grabbed the back of his neck and pushed forward and down until his dipping forehead met my rising knee. There was a muffled thud, and he went limp in my grip. I pulled him through the door and onto the concrete pad, laying him out face down. Luckily he wore shoes with laces. I removed his shoes and then took out the laces. I bound his hands behind his back with one lace, and his ankles together with the other. With Cross helping, I then pulled the body off to the side and dumped him under the bush that grew underneath the window. I didn't think he'd be coming around for a while, and when he did, it would take a while longer for him to get out of the laces. Hopefully by then we'd be finished with what we had to do inside.

Cross followed closely as I entered the tiny living room, which was bare except for a sofa, coffee table, two easy chairs, and low tables at the end of the sofa upon which sat small lamps. Only one lamp was on, which provided little lighting in the room. To the right in the far wall was a door that stood ajar, and I could hear the mumbled hum of voices that were clearly a TV program. Through the crack between the door and the frame I could see a flickering light.

I motioned Cross to be quiet and began moving slowly across the semi-dark living room. At the door, I stood to the side and leaned to peer through the crack with my left eye. Against the room's far wall was an old color console TV. A cartoon was showing. Sitting on the floor in front of the set, dressed in jeans and a short sleeve blue shirt, was a small figure who seemed entranced by the colorful flickering images on the screen. In his hand he clutched a can of cola, and a half-eaten hamburger and greasy packet of fries lay on the floor next to his crossed legs. He was in one quarter profile to me, but I could see enough to catch his resemblance to Christopher Cross. To the right was a clone of the sofa in the living room. I recognized the two men sitting on it as the two I'd followed from Manson's. Both clutched bottles of beer from which they took occasional sips. They were as engrossed in the cartoon as the kid. They didn't exactly have their backs to me, but I had to move quickly and quietly, because it would only take a slight turn of a head for me to be spotted.

The distance from the door to the sofa

looked to be ten feet. The two men sat, not quite touching, but in close proximity to each other. I had to assume they were both armed.

With hand signals I tried to let Cross know I'd go for the two thugs, while he was to grab his son and get him out of the way. He looked confused at first, but eventually got it and bobbed his head up and down in acknowledgement.

Slowly, very slowly, I pushed the door open wide enough for my body to slip through. I eased through the opening and immediately started moving toward the sofa. I could feel Cross coming close behind me.

I'd made it almost to the sofa when the guy on the right turned his head slightly, not looking directly at me, but far enough around that he probably picked up movement in his peripheral vision. His head started turning farther and his mouth opened. I picked up speed, and just as he got turned around far enough to see me, grabbed his left ear. I grabbed the other guy's right ear and slammed their heads together with a cracking sound.

One said 'eep!' The other said 'urk!' Then, they both said 'ow!' in unison.

The kid on the floor looked around, all wide-eyed – not particularly afraid, more like he was curious about the noise. Cross flashed past me. When the kid saw him, he sprang to his feet.

"Daddy," he yelled, and rushed to throw his arms around Cross's legs.

"Calvin," Cross said. "You okay."

"Yeah, I'm okay," the kid said. "I wanta go home."

Cross hugged the boy tightly to him.

I turned my attention back to the two on the sofa, groggy, but still conscious.

Grabbing the smaller of the two, I jerked him over the back of the sofa, held him up with my left hand grasping the collar of his hoodie, and popped him on the bridge of his nose with my right fist. There was a satisfying crunch of bone under my fist and his head bobbed back and forth. Blood spurted from his mashed nose. I released him and his limp form crumpled, falling to a sitting position with his back against the sofa.

I then walked around in front of the sofa where the other guy was sitting shaking his head like a dog shaking off water. His vision must have been blurry still, because he looked up at me, squinting and making 'ngh' sounds through his mouth and nose. I reached down and pulled him up by the collar. He had trouble standing, so I steadied his side-to-side sway by grasping his shoulders. When he was upright, and more or less still, I jammed my stiffened fingers into his solar plexus. He made a 'ngeep' sound and bent forward at the waist. I stopped his forward movement by grabbing his chin and pulling him back upright. When he was again erect I drove my fist into the point of his chin, snapping his head back. His body followed and he went back on the sofa, his hands at his side. Slowly, like syrup flowing over the edge of pancakes, he slid down the sofa to the floor.

I stood there massaging my knuckles.

"Wow," a youthful voice said from my right. "That's just like in the TV show. Daddy, did you see that?"

I turned to see Cross standing there, all goggled eyed, holding his son tightly. The boy had his arms around Cross's neck and was looking at me with a broad smile on his handsome brown face.

"Y-yeah, I saw it son," Cross said. ""You right – it was just like them kung fu dudes on TV."

"I thought I told you to grab the kid and get out of here," I said.

"I was plannin' to, but it was over so fast, I didn't have a chance. What we gone do now?"

"First, we tie these guys up, and then we get the one we left outside back in the house. Then, we call my friend Buster."

19.

Cross wasn't happy when he found out that my friend Buster was a cop.

"Hey, man," he said. "I don't exactly get along too good with the po-leece, you dig."

"If you want to come out of this with your skin intact, you'll have to get along with Detective Mayweather," I said. "He's not just a good cop, he's my best friend. Besides, this is Prince Georges County. He's a District cop with no jurisdiction out here."

"I don't see how me goin' to the fuzz is s'posed to keep Manson off my tail."

I'd changed my mind about Cross after seeing how he was with the boy. He'd risked his life when he learned the kid was in danger, and little Calvin clearly loved him. He was no rocket scientist, though. I sat on the sofa, the three thugs trussed up and stacked in the corner of the room, and he sat on the floor with the boy who was again watching cartoons and seemingly oblivious to all that had only recently transpired. I leaned forward, my palms on my knees and looked at Cross with a stern expression.

"Let me spell it out to you," I said. "As long as Manson's walking free, even if you give the money back to his uncle, he's likely to come after you – or your family. The only way to get rid of that threat is to see him put away."

"Yeah, the law been tryin' to put him away for a long time, but they ain't never been able to make anything stick."

"Until now, you mean. If we can tie him to the kidnapping of your son, he'll go away for a long stretch."

He thought about it for a few minutes. Finally, he agreed. I called Buster and gave him the address.

It took him nearly an hour to get there. In the meantime, we'd watched two cartoons and a stop-motion feature that the kid understood, but was completely over my head, and the three thugs had regained consciousness and were writhing against their restraints in the corner of the room, and cursing up a blue streak. The things they said about my mother caused my cheeks to flame. I'd had to walk over and kick them a time or two to get them to watch their language, reminding them with each kick that there was a child present. They finally gave up and just lay there glaring pure hatred at me.

When Buster rang the bell, I answered the door. Cross was as engrossed in the kiddie show as his kid.

"Okay, bro," Buster said as he walked in. "What's so secret you couldn't tell me over the phone?"

Instead of answering, I took his arm and guided him into the next room. He did a double take and whistled when he saw the three men lying on the floor like so much stacked firewood. His eyebrows shot up when he kept turning and saw Cross sitting on the floor watching TV with his son on his lap.

"Buster," I said. "Allow me to introduce Christopher Cross and his son, Calvin."

Cross eased Calvin to the floor and stood. He looked up at Buster with uncertainty in his eyes.

"Please to meet you," he said.

Buster gave his hand a quick shake and then turned to me.

"Okay, you want to fill me in?"

I filled him in. "If we can tie Manson to snatching the kid, we can take his ass off the street," I said when I'd finished telling him about the case, and what I'd been doing up until the time I called him. "Can you help me do that?"

"I can, but you might not like it," he said. "Actually, your buddy here might not like it."

Cross looked up, his brow furrowed. "Why I got to be involved?" he asked.

"Manson wants your sorry ass," Buster said. "If he thinks he got it, he might say something that'd implicate him. We just have to wire you up so we can get it on tape."

"Whoa, now you just hold on a minute. I ain't gone be talkin' to Augie Manson no how, but 'specially not wearin' a wire. He likely to shoot me before I can get a word in."

"Well, if he did that, we'd get him for murder," Buster said.

Cross's eyes went wide and his lips pursed.

"The idea is that Cross survives this," I said.

"I know," Buster said. "I was just pulling the little rooster's leg. Look, we'd be close by, and soon as Manson admits to taking your boy, we'd move in and arrest him. He's gonna want his money before he does anything serious to you, so all you have to do is let him know you don't have the money on you, but you're willing to take him to it."

Cross looked uncertain, but I thought Buster's proposal made sense.

"I could go in with you," I said. "After all, Manson did offer me money to find you. I can say I had a change of mind."

"I don't know if that's such a good idea, Al," Buster said. "With you there, Manson might not talk too freely."

"He probably right, man," Cross said. "You just a private eye, but you look like the law to somebody like Augie. Maybe your friend right – maybe it'd be better if I go in alone."

I don't know where the little guy got a sudden infusion of guts, but at that moment I was almost proud to know him.

"Don't worry, we'll be real close by," Buster said. "It'll take a coupla hours for me to get a buddy from the precinct to get a wire out here, and I need to call the PG cops to pick these three scum bags up."

He went into the next room and made two calls – the first to a friend in his precinct, asking him to bring a wire and a mobile unit to monitor it, and the second to the Prince

Georges County police, informing them he had three prisoners who had been detained by a citizen to be held for kidnapping a child from the District.

"The PG cops will probably be here first to get these three," he said when he came back into the room. He turned to me. "Al, I think it'll be best if you tell them up front how you came to follow them here and disarmed them."

I hadn't had much contact with the PG authorities, but it made sense. Hopefully they wouldn't be too curious about Cross. I'd just have to leave it to Buster to take care of keeping things cool. Local cops tend to be cooperative with cops from other jurisdictions, but aren't always friendly toward private investigators like me.

The local law arrived within twenty minutes of Buster's call – four county police squad cars with two in each. The senior guy was a sergeant who had worked with Buster previously on a case and liked him, which meant that as a friend of Buster's I was okay in his book. The other seven followed his lead. They brightened up when they saw the bruises on the three thugs, and how I'd trussed them up with their shoe laces. The sergeant gave me a card with an address and number, and asked me to come in and give a formal statement the following day so they could complete the paperwork. He also asked Cross to come in. Cross looked nervous – this was probably the first time in his life he'd spoken to two officers of the law without being arrested. Little Calvin was thoroughly entertained, cartoons, a fight, and now police cars with their flashing lights. An adult would have been completely traumatized after being kidnapped, held in a strange place, and then witnessing as much violence in one evening as this kid had. Children are weird creatures – flexible beyond my ability to understand.

Jake Carson and Manny O'Rourke, two of Buster's friends from his precinct, arrived about five minutes after the PG cops had gone. Carson was a tall, skinny black guy, who kept his head shaved like Buster's, but wore a Fu Manchu mustache and little goatee, and O'Rourke, whose mother was Sicilian, looked more Mediterranean than Irish. O'Rourke carried a small blue bag, from which he pulled a small circular object with three wires attached.

"This is the best we could do at such short notice," he said to Buster, and then turned to me. "Hey, Al, what's up?"

Carson gave me a fist at shoulder Black Power salute and a broad smile.

"Yeah, bro," he said. "What trouble you

got our man Buster in now?"

With Cross and the kid in the next room watching TV, I sat them on the couch in the living room and gave them a summary of the case. Buster then outlined what we planned to do to get Manson.

"We got a warrant to do this?" Carson asked. "Because if we don't, anything we pick up will get thrown out of court."

"No, Cross has consented to wear a wire and let his conversation be recorded," Buster said. "So, no warrant is needed. Everything we get can be used."

"He's right on that," O'Rourke said. "So, what we need is for this guy Cross to get Manson talking, and have him admit he ordered the boy's kidnapping, right? You sure he's up to it?"

"He looks a little squirrelly," I said. "But, he's a pit bull when it comes to that kid. Besides, he's a con man, I think he'll be okay."

"I don't suppose you're gonna tell us how this dude Cross got connected with Manson," Carson said. He didn't even bother to phrase it as a question.

"Let's just say Cross did something Manson didn't like, so he snatched his kid to get back at him," Buster said, saving me from having to answer. "Right now, our job's to get a scum bag off the street that has children kidnapped. We been trying to take Manson down for years. This is finally our chance to do it."

"Okay then," O'Rourke said. "Let's get Cross wired."

That got a laugh from everyone, including Cross. Little Calvin just looked puzzled until Cross explained that they were doing this to get the bad man who'd had him taken from his school. That brought a bright smile to his young face.

"Yeah, we get the bad man." He looked at me. "You donna do some more kung fu?"

Charles Ray

20.

Watching Cross getting the wire attached to his body was even more entertaining to little Calvin than the cartoons had been.

It seems Cross was ticklish, and every time O'Rourke touched him he folded over giggling, which started Calvin giggling, and pretty soon had all of us holding our sides.

"Come on, man," O'Rourke said. "This is gonna take all night if you don't sit still."

Cross wiped his eyes. "Sorry, but your hands are cold."

O'Rourke rubbed his hands together briskly.

"Okay, now hold still while I tape these antenna wires in place."

He'd placed the transmitter, a quarter-inch-thick round plastic device that was four inches in diameter, under Cross's left pectoral, not quite under his arm, taping it in place with transparent plastic tape. That little operation had started the giggling, but when he began taping the antenna wires down his left side, it got crazy. It took some doing, but it was finally done.

"Will that thing work around to the side like that?" I asked.

"It's pretty sensitive," O'Rourke said. "It'll pick up any normal conversation within three or four feet. Problem is, it won't transmit far. Our van's gonna have to be within two blocks to be able to pick up the signal."

I described the area, suggesting they park the van on the parallel street behind Manson's building. That would put them less than a block away, but out of sight of anyone who might be watching the street in front of the place.

"Are you sure we have enough manpower for this?" I asked.

"Good point," Buster said. "Manson's likely to have a buncha his goons in the place. I'll call a few more guys from the precinct."

He made a few more calls. When he explained why he was calling, he had no problem getting volunteers – including a couple of off-duty guys.

"Okay," he said after hanging up from the last call. "We'll have ten additional guys. I told 'em to meet us behind Manson's place in two hours."

"That gives us time to drop Calvin off at his mom's," I said. I turned to Cross. "Then you and I have to go over your role. You ready for this?"

"Yeah, I guess so." He didn't sound as convincing as I'd have liked, but we were committed.

I took him and the boy in my car with Buster following, while the other two cops drove their van to scout the area behind Manson's.

The reunion, when we arrived at Kaine's apartment, involved a lot of tears, hugging, and kissing. Cross apologized for putting them in danger. Kaine said if he ever ran away like that again *she'd* kill him. Calvin just wanted to talk about the way I'd beat the three bad men like in the Kung Fu movies. Kaine wasn't too thrilled when she learned of our plan, but Cross convinced her it was the only way to remove the man as a threat to them.

As we were leaving, she pulled me aside.

"If anything happens to him, I'm holding

you responsible," she said.

"Don't you worry. I'll stick to him like a tick on a horse's rump."

She looked confused, and then she smiled. "You better."

Cross rode with me as we followed Buster's Pontiac to the street behind Manson's place. He pulled in behind the unmarked blue van, and I stopped directly behind him.

We got out and joined Buster beside his car. Up ahead I saw four other unmarked cars. They were all empty. I assumed that Buster's friends were concealed in the shadows of the vacant lot nearby, ready to move on his signal.

"You ready to do this?" Buster asked.

Cross swallowed hard and bobbed his head up and down. I put a hand on his shoulder. "Don't worry," I said. "Buster and his guys are right here, and I'll be in the parking lot next to the building."

"That's not a bad idea," Buster said. "Hang on, and I'll move everybody to the parking lot." He took his radiophone from his pocket. "Manny, can you hear me?"

"Loud and clear, boss," O'Rourke's voice came back. "Just got called from Carl and

Jacob. They heard what was going down and are coming in their squad cars. Over."

"Good. Have 'em hold up at both ends of the block in front, and move in on my signal. Break. Deke, you got your ears on?"

"Yeah, boss, come back." The voice was tinny, and a bit garbled.

"Coming your way with two people," Buster said. "Get ready to move closer. We're launching from the parking lot beside the building."

"We got eyes on you. Come on," the voice said.

Buster put the radio back. "Okay," he said. "Let's move out."

We crossed the trash-strewn vacant lot. As we reached the service road that ran the length of the block behind the buildings on Manson's block, several dark figures rose from hiding places and fell in behind us. When we reached the edge of the parking lot, Buster motioned them to the perimeter and we hugged the corner of the building. I turned to Cross.

"You're on," I said. "Just remember to stay calm. Try to get Manson talking. Soon as he admits to the kidnapping, we're coming in. Got it?"

"Yeah, got it," Cross said. "Just don't be late."

He took a deep breath and walked along the wall toward the front of the building. With one last look over his shoulder, he disappeared around the corner.

Buster, his back against the wall beside me, pulled his service weapon from its hip holster. "Nothing we can do now but wait," he said.

Waiting's always the hard part. You start thinking about all the things that can go wrong. I found myself worrying that Manson would have Cross shot down the moment he entered the place, even though that was highly unlikely to happen until *after* he got his money back. The seconds crawled by with the speed of cold molasses. I hate the waiting.

"Boss, Manny here," O'Rourke's voice came from Buster's pocket. "Manson just admitted to the kidnapping."

I doubt if that he'd literally done that, but obviously he'd said something that would link him to the kidnapping in the mind of a cop, which was enough for me. Even before Buster could say 'go' into the radio, I was sprinting around the corner toward the front. I heard feet scuffling the gravel of the parking lot behind me.

I spun around the corner, ran to the door and slammed it open. The same two guys from earlier were there. I ignored the small one behind the table, and launched myself at Muscles, my left foot slamming into his solar plexus and sending him tumbling through the curtain into the main room. He landed on his back, and I stepped on his chest, kicking him in the chin, almost losing my balance in the process. Stepping off him, I looked around. Augie Manson was near the right end of the bar, his meaty hands grasping the collars of Cross's polo shirt. I sprinted in that direction.

Pandemonium erupted as a dozen cops lead by Buster flooded through the curtains behind me and spread out across the front of the room with their guns drawn.

"Nobody move," Buster shouted in that booming voice of his. "This is a raid. Augie Manson, you're under arrest for kidnapping."

Most of the patrons were edging back toward the walls. A few moved hands nervously toward pockets, looking to Manson for direction. He turned and smiled at Buster, motioning his men to stand down.

"Well now, officer," he said. "This is a private establishment, and if you don't have a warrant, you're trespassing. As to that ridiculous charge of kidnapping, upon what do you base it? Who am I supposed to have kidnapped?"

Buster took out his radio. "Manny, you want to play Manson's confession back?"

He turned the volume up and held the device up. The voices were low, but clear and recognizable.

"I'll get your money," Cross's voice said. "You got to let my boy go home."

"Okay," Manson's voice came back. "You stay here, and I'll call my men and tell them to take the brat home."

Buster turned the radio off and returned it to his pocket. "Enough evidence for you?" he asked.

Manson turned to Cross, his fleshy face contorted with rage. "You son of a bitch. You're wearing a wire."

Cross smiled and before anyone could stop him, he hit Manson squarely on the nose, causing a gusher of blood to spew from it. The big man squealed and stumbled backwards, his hands over his nose.

"That's for snatching my boy, you bastard," Cross said. Then, he kicked Manson in the crotch, causing him to drop to his knees, one hand over his nose, the other over his aching balls. "And, that's for upsetting my woman."

"Now, that's gotta hurt," Buster said.

Charles Ray

21.

Buster had Manson hauled away in cuffs. The two cops escorting him had to support him because he was still wobbly from the kick Cross had given him. He looked around the room, as if daring any of Manson's men to do something. That many armed cops wearing armored vests, with the business end of service revolvers and assault rifles pointe their way was a pretty intimidating sight. There were no takers.

As we were walking back to our vehicles, Cross put a hand on my arm. "Thanks, man. You too, Detective Mayweather," he said.

"Thank you for helping us get Manson," Buster said. "I got a question, though. What was that about you getting Manson his money back?"

"It was a gambling debt," I said. I don't

like telling lies to Buster, but I didn't want Cross to have to lie. If he told Buster the truth, he might have to arrest him for fraud. Candace Kaine wouldn't like that. The things I do for clients. Cross gave me a look of gratitude.

"You shouldn't be hooking up with lowlifes like that," Buster said. "What kinda example that set for that boy of yours?"

"You're right," Cross said. "That life's behind me now. No more sca-, er gambling for me."

"And, stay out of places like this. I'm gonna have to tip narcotics off to raid the place. I smelled pot in the air, and I'll bet they got other drugs behind the bar too."

"Oh, I ain't never done no drugs," Cross said. "Nothin' stronger than a Scotch straight up now and then."

"Okay, you two follow me back to the precinct after we take that wire off you. I'm gonna need both your statements." Buster grinned broadly. "This is gonna look good on my sheet. I brought down Augie Manson."

"You are the man," I said.

At the precinct, Buster had Cross and me sit in one of the interview rooms and write our statements on legal pads. Mine was considerably longer, since I had to explain how I'd crossed paths with Manson in the first place. I quietly advised Cross to leave out Manson's uncle, and just say that he owed Manson a large sum of money, which is why, in his opinion, Manson had his son kidnapped. Technically, it wasn't untrue. I don't know why I was going out of my way to protect Cross, except for the fact that when it counted he'd stepped up. He'd taken responsibility for his actions. He walked into Manson's place, knowing the man could well have killed him out of hand. That took guts. He'd never be on my Christmas list – not that I have a Christmas list – but I'd developed a little respect for him. He wasn't a totally lost cause.

I'm a firm believer, though, in trust but verify. To make sure he didn't go back on his word, I had Cross take me to where he'd stashed his money – a rundown apartment building not too far from the apartment he shared with Kaine and the boy. He'd hidden it in the lumpy mattress of the cramped one-bedroom apartment he was renting by the day, a total of one hundred fifty thousand dollars. After giving Seymour Wilson his hundred grand back, he'd still be left with a tidy sum. He'd probably scammed some other poor suckers for it, but I didn't know them, and they weren't likely to have nephews who were gangsters to come after him, so I decided to look the other way.

I drove him out to Seat Pleasant, to Wilson's place. The old man was happy to get his money back, but that happiness was countered by my news that his nephew was now a resident of a holding cell at DC metro police.

"He ain't gone be there long," he said. "And, when he get out, he gone fix your ass, Cross."

"I don't think he'll be getting out soon," I said. "They got him for kidnapping. He confessed to it on tape no less."

"Who he kidnap?"

"My son," Cross said. "He's only six years old. Ain't right puttin' a little kid like that through that, you know. I hope they lock his ass away for good."

"In prison, the other convicts don't care too much for people who hurt kids," I added. I left the rest unsaid. Wilson understood what I meant, but his concern for his nephew was outweighed by the site of a hundred grand in crumpled bills spread out on his coffee table.

We left him sitting on his couch counting his money.

22.

A week after everything went down, I was sitting in my office with nothing much to do. I'd just tracked down a missing heiress to a tract of land in Wyoming – found her hanging out in a religious commune near Petersburg, Virginia, and when I gave her the letter informing her that she was now a very rich woman she took and tore it into shreds. She calmly pissed away somewhere in the neighborhood of fifty million dollars, smiling as she did it. Didn't leave me much to do but come back to Washington and report to Quincy Chang. This was one of the things I did for Holcombe, Stein and Chang, the firm of which Quincy was a partner, and how I earned my ten thousand dollar monthly retainer. He took it in stride, thanked me, and that was that. I was bored.

Heather walked into my office. "Hey, boss, you got visitors," she said.

She stepped aside and ushered Christopher Cross, Candace Kaine, and her son Calvin into my office. The boy looked none the worse for his recent experience. When he saw me he ran over and stuck out his hand. I gripped warmly and shook.

"Hey there, little man," I said. "What have you been up to?"

"I'm going to a new school," he said.

"Oh, what was wrong with the old school?"

"It's too far from our new house."

I looked up at the two adults who stood there arm in arm beaming like newlyweds. Then I noticed the simple gold band on Kaine's left ring finger.

"Did you two-"

"We got married two days ago," Kaine said, holding the ring up for me to see.

Cross just looked smug.

"And, you got a new house," I said.

"Yeah," he said. "I figured it was a good use for the money I had left."

I stood and extended my hand. He grasped it and held on for a while.

"I'm happy for you, for all three of you," I said. "Where's the new house?"

"It's in Largo," Kaine said. "Not too far from the Metro, so Chris and I can take the train downtown to work."

I looked at him with raised eyebrows.

"Yeah, that friend of yours, Detective Mayweather helped me get a job. I'm a mail clerk at this office building near L'Enfant Plaza," he said. "It don't pay much, but with two paychecks, we can get by okay."

"We have you to thank for it," Kaine said. "Us being together as a family, the new house, Chris's job – if not for you none of this would've happened."

"Don't sell yourselves short. Chris came back and stood up like a man when the chips were down." He blushed. "It took guts for him to face Manson like he did. And you, well, you never quit believing in him, and that's important. Everyone has to have someone who believes in them, right, Calvin?" I rumpled the boy's curly hair.

"Yeah, but I want to learn to fight like you do," he said.

"Now, Calvin, what has mommy told you about fighting?"

"Aw, mom," he said. "You shoulda seen it.

He whipped two guys with his hands just like the ninjas on TV."

"Boy's got a point, babe," Cross said. "It was something to see. Actually, he took out three armed dudes with his bare hands. And, you shoulda seen what he did to that big dude at Manson's – kicked him down and then stomped on his face, and he was near twice Mr. Pennyback's size."

"What am I to do with these two?" Kaine said, looking at me with that pained look mothers can get sometimes.

I shrugged.

"Boys will be boys," I said. "Look, congratulations to you guys. I'd like to give you a little combination wedding and house warming present."

"That's not necessary," she said. "You've already done enough for us."

"That was my job. This is different. As a present, I'm writing off the rest of the money you owe me."

"Wow," Cross said.

"I don't know what to say, or how to thank you," Kaine said. "You must come to our house warming by the way. We're having it this weekend if you're free. And, Heather is invited too. I assume a good looking man like you has a girlfriend, so she's included as well. We invited that nice Detective Mayweather and his family, and he already accepted."

Sandra and I hadn't made any weekend plans, and she's such a sucker for love stories I was sure she'd love it. "Sure, just let Heather know the time and address."

Candace Kaine hugged me and kissed me on the cheek. Cross shook my hand, giving it an extra manly squeeze. Calvin Kaine, now Cross, also shook my hand and asked if when I came to the party I'd teach him some kung fu, which earned him another frown from his mother. They left my office with Calvin between them holding their hands.

I sat back behind my desk. I was no longer bored. Life was good.

23.

Their house was not far from Largo Town Center. A small ranch style house with a one-car garage on a small lot in a new community with an elementary school just two blocks away – the suburban dream for first time home buyers.

I pulled into the driveway, got out and held the door for Sandra who was carrying a large chocolate cake she'd picked up at the bakery in Potomac Village while I carried a bottle of red wine from my stock. I'd told her about my gift, but she insisted we should arrive with presents.

Candace Kaine, wearing a brown one-piece dress that made her look like the typical suburban housewife, met us at the door. When we walked into the small, but tastefully furnished living room, I was attacked by a whirling dervish. Calvin attached himself to my right leg.

"You gonna teach me kung fu now?" he asked.

"Not now, Calvin," Kaine said. "Let Mr. Pennyback get his breath and have something to drink first."

Then, Calvin got a look at Sandra and the cake she was carrying. I'm not sure what attracted him most, her astonishing good looks, or the rich chocolate cake, but he let go of my lets and planted himself in front of her, looking up with an angelic smile on his face.

"Is that cake for me?" he asked. "It's not my birthday yet. You're pretty."

The kid had good eyes, though. I had to give him that. Kaine gave Sandra a pained look accompanied by a shrug.

"I'm sorry, Ms. Winter," she said. "He's at that age where his mind jumps from one thing to another with the speed of light. Calvin, honey, why don't you take Mr. Pennyback out to the patio so he can get a drink? Ms. Winter, could I impose on you to help me in the kitchen?"

"Only if you call me Sandra. You have a beautiful house."

And just like that, they became Sandra

and Candy, as if they'd known each other for years. They linked arms and headed for that magic domain of women in the suburbs, the kitchen, while Calvin took my hand and began pulling me toward one of the few places men in the 'burbs are allowed to rule – the patio. I found Cross doing what millions of suburban men do on weekends in warm weather besides mow lawns – standing in front of a grill wearing a silly apron waiting for the charcoal to get to the right temperature.

"Mr. Pennyback," he said when Calvin and I came through the sliding glass door from the living room. "Glad you could come. I got beers in the cooler over there. Help yourself."

"Can I have a drink too, daddy?" the kid asked, jumping up and down.

Cross rolled his eyes. "Okay, buddy. You mind pulling a soda out for Calvin, Mr. Pennyback?"

"No problem," I said. "By the way, you can call me Al. Job's over." I took an orange soda from the cooler, opened it and handed it to Calvin, and then took out a can of beer for myself.

While Calvin slurped orange soda, getting as much on his face and shirt as down his mouth, I engaged in small talk with his father. Cross seemed to be taking to suburban life.

As I sat there on a folding lawn chair watching Cross grill hot dogs and beef patties, my mind drifted back to similar scenes from my own life. Of course, the back yard had belonged to a modest house in one of the officer housing areas on Fort Bragg, North Carolina. My son, Ethan, had been about the age of Calvin. He was just as rambunctious, and like Calvin, adored his father. I could feel a stinging sensation in my eyes as the memories came flooding back - Ethan and I on the patio grilling steaks while Sarah fixed potato salad in the kitchen.

My reverie was interrupted by the swishing sound of the patio door sliding open. Buster walked through, followed by the twins, little Albert and Sandra. They'd reached the age where they were talking, running, climbing on everything they could reach, and testing the limits of adult authority. They bumped into Buster's legs when he stopped, peering around at me, Calvin, and Cross.

Cross was a strange adult, and they had very little interest in strange adults. Me, of course, they knew, and whenever I visited their house they'd swarm all over me, wanting to be tickled or tossed in the air. But, Calvin was a new phenomenon. He was larger than them, but not quite adult size – a novelty. The eased from behind Buster and walked over to face him. He smiled. They smiled. He invited them to play on the slide located just off the patio. Their smiles widened, and the three of them darted off.

"Looks like Albert and Sandra just made a new friend," Buster said. "Hey, Chris, you got the place looking good. How's the job going?"

"Thanks, Detective Mayweather. I been workin' on the place ever chance I get. The job goin' fine. Thank you for helpin' me get it."

"You keep it up, and you'll be fine." He turned to me. "Hey, bro, any more beer 'round here?" I pulled a can from the cooler and tossed it to him. He popped the tab and took a long drink. "You two'll be glad to know that Augie Manson's likely to go down for a long count for kidnapping Calvin. They're goin' for a life sentence."

"I didn't realize the District had such stiff penalties," I said.

"Ain't the District goin' after him. He screwed up by having his goons take the kid to Maryland. When they took the kid out of the District, they made it a federal crime. The Justice Department's been after Manson for racketeering for a long time, and they insisted on prosecuting him under the Lindberg Law."

He was referring to the federal law that was passed after the 1932 kidnapping and murder of the 18-month old son of the famous aviator Charles Lindbergh. When Bruno Hauptmann was found guilty of the crime and executed at the New Jersey State Prison in 1936, the public and media outcry was so shrill, congress passed the Federal Kidnapping Act, known as the Lindbergh Law, making transporting a kidnapping victim across state lines a federal crime, with the possibility of a life sentence if convicted.

"Are they going for a life sentence?" I asked.

"Bet your ass they are, and that dude's as good as convicted. The Prince Georges County guys got statements from the three turkeys we turned over. When they found out Manson had been arrested, they started singing like a boys' choir. They're turning state's evidence in exchange for lighter sentences. The U.S. Attorney's going for the max against Manson, though."

"Couldn't happen to a nicer guy," Cross said.

"I guess this'll put a crimp in his criminal enterprise," I said.

Buster made a snorting sound. "Nah – there'll be somebody else stepping up to fill his shoes, if there ain't already. Too much money involved."

"That for sure," Cross said. "People be greedy – always lookin' for the big score. That's why I was able to make it long's I did. Everbody want to get something for as close to nothin' as possible."

Buster looked at him with narrowed eyes. "I hope you ain't thinking about going back to that life, boy?"

"Oh, no sir – not me. I come close to losin' my woman and my boy. That taught me a lesson 'bout what really matter. It be nice to be rich, but long's I got the two of them, I figure I'm 'bout as rich as I need to be."

"Lots of money to be made out there on the streets, you know," Buster said. "It can be mighty tempting."

Cross put the spatula he was holding on the rack attached to the side of the grill, and turned to face Buster, looking up at him with a pugnacious expression on his face. "I know that," he said. "I know that better than you think. I also know that I got a responsibility to Candy, but most of all, I got a responsibility to my son." His expression softened and he looked at Calvin who was playing with the twins on the slide. "My momma died right after giving birth to me, and my grandma say my daddy brought me to her place and then hit the road. I ain't never laid eyes on nothin' more'n a picture of him in my life. When I was growin' up the one thing I swore I'd never be was a deadbeat dad, and I swore that again when Calvin was born."

"Yeah, but you were planning to run out on 'em," Buster said insistently.

"I know it looks like that – but, when I found out I'd crossed Augie Manson, I just thought if I put some distance between me and them they'd be safe. I was wrong about that, and I know it now."

"He *did* come back," I said.

"I know," Buster said. "And, I salute him for that. I'm just makin' sure he means to stay this time."

"You can be damn sure of it," Cross said. "This whole thing done taught me a lesson. You can't run away from your responsibility, you got to face it square no matter how bad it seems. I'd die for that boy and his momma. You gotta believe that."

Buster smiled and put a beefy hand on Cross's shoulder. "I believe you, kid," he said. "I just had to hear you say it."

I wondered if Cross understood just how close he'd come to doing what he said he was willing to do. Maybe he did, maybe not, but he'd shown us – and himself – that he wasn't a deadbeat dad. In the end, that was all that counted.

The rest of the day was a typical happy day in the suburbs.

Charles Ray

24.

On Sunday, Sandra and I slept in. We got up at ten, did a quick run through the woods, showered, and made a light brunch which we ate sitting on the back porch.

The early heat had abated. The weather was perfect for al fresco dining, with a slight breeze blowing in from the south, rustling the leaves of the trees making a sound like a light rain on a tile roof. A herd of five deer led by an old doe grazed at the edge of the forest, stopping from time to time to eye Sandra and me warily. Satisfied, though, that the two of us posed no threat, the animals came nearer and nearer the porch.

Our meal finished, we sat back enjoying a second cup of coffee and each other's company.

"Did you have a good time yesterday?" I asked.

Charles Ray

She looked at me over the rim of her coffee cup. "You know I did. Candy and Chris have a nice house."

"Yeah, looks like he's turned his life around."

She laid a soft hand on mine, moving her index finger around in small circles. I felt a tingling sensation that wasn't at all unpleasant. "I think they'll work out," she said. "They clearly love each other very much."

"And, love conquers all," I said, with a bit more sarcasm than I intended.

She pinched the back of my hand. It didn't hurt – just a little sting like a mosquito bite.

"Don't knock it," she said. "True love can help people overcome obstacles. Chris loves Candy and Calvin. That's what made him come back despite the danger to himself. That's what will make it possible for the two of them to bridge their differences."

"I suppose you have a point, but I think it was more a sense of responsibility that made him come back." I told her the story Cross had told me about his father. "He's determined to be a better man than his father, and accept his responsibility."

"And, you don't think love has anything to

178

do with it?"

I shrugged. I hadn't really thought about it that much.

"I suppose there's really no simple answer, is there?"

She put her cup on the table and got up from her chair. Easing herself onto my lap, she put her arms around my neck and laid her head against my shoulder. The grazing deer were soon forgotten.

Turns out there is a simple answer after all.

Al Pennyback mysteries

Color Me Dead
Memorial to the Dead
Deadline
Dead, White, and Blue
A Good Day to Die
The Day the Music Died
Die, Sinner
Deadly Intentions
Death by Design
Till Death Do Us Part
Deadly Dose
Dead Man's Cove
Dead Men Don't Answer
Deadly Paradise
Kiss of Death
Death in White Satin
Death and Taxis
Deadbeat

Other books by this author:
The Buffalo Soldier series:

Buffalo Soldier: Trial by Fire
Buffalo Soldier: Homecoming
Buffalo Soldier: Incident at Cactus Junction
Buffalo Soldier: Peacekeepers
Buffalo Soldier: Renegade
Buffalo Soldier: Escort Duty
Buffalo Soldier: Yosemite
Buffalo Soldier: Battle at Dead Man's Gulch

Other fiction

Angel on His Shoulder
She's No Angel
Child of the Flame
Pip's Revenge
Wallace in Underland
Further Adventures of Wallace in Underland
Dead Letter and Other Tales
The Last Gunfighters
The Culling
The White Dragons
The Dragon's Lair
Dragon Slayer
Frontier Justice

Nonfiction

Things I Learned from My Grandmother About Leadership and Life
Taking Charge: Effective Leadership for the Twenty-first Century
Grab the Brass Ring
There's Always a Plan B
African Places: A Photographic Journey Through Zimbabwe and southern Africa
A Portrait of Africa

About the Author

Charles Ray has been writing fiction since his teens. He won a Sunday school magazine writing contest when he was thirteen, and having his byline on a short story published in a national publication forever hooked him on writing. During his time in the army (1962-1982) he often moonlighted as a newspaper or magazine journalist, and was the editorial cartoonist for the Spring Lake (NC) News, a weekly newspaper, during the 1970s. In addition to his writing, he was an artist/cartoonist and photographer for a number of publications, including Ebony, Eagle and Swan, and Essence, and had a monthly cartoon feature and did several covers for Buffalo, a now-defunct magazine that was dedicated to showcasing the contributions of African-Americans to the country's military history.

After retiring from the army, he joined the U.S. Foreign Service, and served as a diplomat in posts in Asia and Africa until his retirement in 2012. He has worked and traveled throughout the world (Antarctica is the only continent he hasn't visited), and now, as a full time writer, continues to globetrot looking for interesting things to write about, draw, or take pictures of.

A native of Texas, he now calls Maryland home. For more on his writing and other projects, check one of the following Web sites:

http://redroom.com/member/charles-a-ray
http://charlesaray.blogspot.com
http://charlieray45.wordpress.com
http://www.twitter.com/charlieray45
http://www.facebook.com/charlieray45
http://www.flickr.com/photos/charlesray45/
http://www.viewbug.com/member/charlesray

www.ingramcontent.com/pod-product-compliance
Lightning Source LLC
Chambersburg PA
CBHW060156130626
46556CB00006B/2665